MYRIAD HUES: A SELECTION OF SHORT STORIES BY

ARUN GOSWAMI

Translated From Assamese Into English By Subhajit Bhadra

TRUE SIGN
PUBLISHING HOUSE

Published by True Sign Publishing House
Address: SY. No. 21/2 & 21/3, Sonnenahalli,
Krishnarajapura, Bengaluru,
Karnataka - 560049 India
E-mail: truesignbooks@gmail.com
Website: www.truesign.in

Myriad Hues: A Selection Of Short Stories
By Arun Goswami

Translated From Assamese Into English
By Subhajit Bhadra

ISBN: 978-93-5584-846-8

First Edition: 2023

CONTENTS

Preface

In the cultural and literal domain of Assam, Arun Goswami has carved a niche for himself. He has penned short stories, novels, novelettes and plays with equal aplomb and elan. Arun Goswami is a writer with immense social consciousness and he does not merely extract from the readers approval of social atrocity, he compels them to believe that they are also part of it. Arun Goswami has written almost one thousand stories, from which twenty three stories have been selected for this anthology. To choose Arun's Goswami's stories is a daunting task because they are full of variety and hues. So this collection is also a maiden and the first of its kind as for the first time his stories are being translated from Assamese language into English. Translation in the literal sense is never possible as the various cultural nuances cannot be transferred or converted from one language into another. Arun Goswami has written stories based on Assam's various rural places and he uses typical colloquial expression and that is why the English translation has been very difficult. However, with the liberty given to me by the author, I have been able to translate the stories in peace and transcreation has become possible. Now, the readers would decide how far this venture is successful.

Translator's Preface

Arun Goswami is one of those bold and courageous Assamese writers who has consistently engaged himself in addressing contemporary socio-political issues of his time. Arun Goswami has exhibited his prowess in different literary genres such as the novel, short story and essay with equal aplomb. There is a thin, but subtle difference between socio-awareness and socio-responsibility and Goswami has always been able to strike a successful balance between the two. There are many writers who find it very difficult to maintain a healthy relation between quality and quantity, but it is to Arun Goswami's credit that in spite of being a prolific writer, he has always been able to produce quality writing. Good literature must evoke the qualities of sensitivity and compassion which Goswami excels in doing. He strikes a nice balance between subject matter and style and he does not believe in unnecessary embellishment. His style is lucid, bare and his narrative is free-flowing.

As regards Goswami's method, he follows the realistic mode perfected by the classical French masters and most of his works are true to the chosen surroundings. He portrays with breathtaking effect the panic, dread and anxiety in the minds of the ordinary villagers who helplessly find themselves at the receiving end of a brutal and inhuman army operation. Goswami brilliantly depicts how the ordinary villagers were harassed and humiliated by the army, how many youths were lifted to the army camp without showing any proper reason, how the old and helpless were beaten mercilessly and how the women were raped by the army jawans. Goswami provides an authentic picture of that dark phase which characterized the state of Assam at a very critical juncture and his success lies in creating a realistic portrait of a village plagued by dread, horror and death, without reducing it to the level of a documentary. Goswami's novel becomes significant in the context that not many Assamese writers ventured into the daring territory of exploring the dark and sombre phase of the state. The novel ultimately exhibits how ordinary civilians start rebelling against every oppressive machinery of the state and exemplifies their extreme courage, determination and grit to live in the midst of death and violence that paralyse ordinary lives.

In **Aai Bortoman**, Arun Goswami deals with his favourite domain - the depiction of a turbulent phase of Assam, that reduced it to the level of an extremely volatile zone. That Assam witnessed a major upheaval during the 1980s and 1990s due to the rise of violent insurgency is known to everybody. That many ideologically inclined youths left the comfort and security of the four walls of his home in order to erase poverty, deprivation and inequality, coupled with corruption deeply rooted in the state machinery is also known to many. That these bright and brilliant dreams come to naught in the subsequent period - once the members associated with this visionary distance themselves from their main ideology and converted this massive force into an insurgency group, killing innocent people, is also known to many. That the security forces deployed later on by the central government to tame the insurgents and the subsequent reign of terror that prevailed in the minds of the ordinary civilians is also known to many. But Arun Goswami's, **Aai Bortoman** provides a vivid and stunning picture of a remote village of Assam which is torched by the army in search of insurgents. Goswami's short story, **Hagunor Kho** captures through the metaphor of a vulture, the harsh and deplorable life of a social underdog who takes care of dead bodies, but the irony of the story lies in the fact that when he dies, there is no one to take care of his dead body and the author's sympathy is with this socially despised character, who exhibited human feelings whenever the situation so demanded.

In **Moraghoria**, Arun Goswami poignantly portrays the pathetic life of a family dogged by acute poverty, where the son of a just deceased father is delighted, thinking about the ritual of bringing food items to the home of a dead person as it would relieve his hunger.

Manuhbor Pagolne Pagolbor Manooh explores the vulgar and brutal mass psyche through the evocative tale of two mad women who become dependent on each other and the sympathy of the narrator lies with these mad women as is evident in the ironic and sarcastic title of the story.

Nangoth Posak explores through the framework of a madman's tale the nakedness of the morally bankrupt people who have reduced human society to the level of a whorehouse, where everything can be bought and sold in terms of money, where there is no human warmth and where there is hardly any sign of compassion and fellow feeling.

Putonar Amrit Stan is an extremely evocative tale of the hatred and love that is executed through the framework of an ethnic clash between two different communities of Assam, where a couple first decides to kill the son of their enemy in a brutal manner, but ultimately adopts that very child, realizing the futility of violence.

Gorioborta Marikhali vividly brings to light the inhuman treatment of the social underdogs in the hands of the so-called upper-class, who suffer from no moral qualities, taking advantage of their helplessness. It also deals with the theme of communal harmony and it, in fact, becomes the central crux of the piece when Kamal, the protagonist who happens to be a Hindu, pays tribute to the elderly Muslim man who became a victim to a fabricated communal riot.

Premor Hongya is an extremely poignant tale of a cobbler who preserves the memory of his dead wife long after her death and the existence of the husband becomes meaningful through the genuine love he still feels for his deceased wife. It is precisely this aspect which intrigues the educated narrator, who compares this unconditional love that is pure with the strife-ridden and hypocritical married lives of many sophisticated urban people and the love of the cobbler appears to the narrator to be a redemptive force in today's selfish world.

In **Moi Muk Herualu** (I have lost myself), Arun Goswami deals with an individual's trauma of losing his vital essence as a human being as he compromises with all the prevailing corruption and injustice that plagues the society and immediate surroundings. It is a novel which brings to light how the contemporary society around us has been contaminated to such a degree that it has become an almost impossible task for the honest human individual to retain his/her integrity. The novel also mercilessly exposes the compromising mentality of those people who put individual profit over every other concern.

There is a symbiotic relationship between Arun Goswami's short stories and his novels. The stories seem to be footnotes to his novels. His stories remind of Norman Mailer and the letter's Tropic of Cancer.

While translating the stories, utmost care has been taken to ensure variety. Exact literal translation was not possible and that is why transcreation was aimed at. The stories acquire a different resonance after being translated. We don't want to make any claims but it is a fact that the charm of the original has been retained. Arun Goswami might appear fresh through translation.

What is heartening is that Arun Goswami's works are translated into English for the first time. The rest is for the readers to judge.

In the literary and cultural horizon of Assam, Arun Goswami is a familiar name. His writings reflect social awareness and he has always launched a crusade against social oppression. His field of creation is broader and recently he has brought glory to Assam by being the author of the largest book of the World, published by Chandra Prakash, Assam. He has written stories like "**Masmoria Soalir Laj,**" "**Ai Kot Nai**" and others based on which critically acclaimed movies have been made. Based on Dergaon literature is Goswami's vocation. He has also written successful plays and serials for television. Arun Goswami is a committed writer and this is his first collection of Assamese short stories in English translation

Bad People

It was obvious from his face that Amar had not been able to sleep for the last few days. There were wrinkles on his face. He gave a faded smile. If he got anxious or sad he kept quiet. He had not gone anywhere for the last three days and most of the time he spent sitting in the verandah. His decision forced other members of the house to keep quiet. His quietness discouraged his brothers from giving any advice. Amar had almost finalized his decision.

One day Kiran aunty asked him, "Is it true Amar that you are going tomorrow? I have slightly heard the rumour. Now, Junu has told me that you are going. What are you going to do?" Amar just passed a smile and said nothing. She asked Amar's sister-in-law, "Why do you let him go?" The sister-in-law too replied nothing. Amar's three-year-old son came near Kiran aunty and said, "Grandma, we are going tomorrow. Don't you know?"

"Why are you leaving us?"

The boy did not wait to reply and ran to his uncle and jumped into his lap. While running he stumbled on the bell-metal tray used to offer betel-nuts.

Kiran aunty said, "We felt proud. Everyone runs towards the city after getting a job. But after so many years you have come back to the village. We felt proud my son. All of them who have a job like yours live in the city. You came back to the village on your own accord and we felt proud for it. No one can deny your contribution to the village." Kiran aunty could not finish the sentence. Amar's wife, Archi handed over a cup of tea to her and said,"Aunty, please don't insist anymore. He will be mad if he stays here. He is such a meek person."

"Amar has helped me a lot. After the death of their uncle my nephews never cared for me. Instead of helping me they started backbiting. With the two young girls how do they mange the house? They even raise eyebrows even if a young relative comes to our house. I have been toiling hard to earn something and they instead of helping, blames us. Amar is not my kith and kin, yet he helped me a lot to get the Government aid. Only because of that aid I could start my business and can live with respect. I did not have to go anywhere else for the aid. I have seen people going to unwanted persons for help. They would slap me for saying all these but the truth can't be hidden."

"That's the problem," Archi said, "Those people you have mentioned just now are the prominent persons of the village. They keep the people moving on their fingertips. For how long will they rule ? Everyone knows the truth. It's just their fear that stops people from reacting."

"He had been sad for a few days. It had been twenty years since independence, still these roads were in poor condition. No one could force the authorities to build a culvert. All the higher sections of the society like the teacher, overseer, clerk, officer, etc. travelled by this road, yet no one cut the tree down and cleared the road. He had worked for the development of the village. He had established a cooperative society and a school, had developed the library, arranged safe drinking water. But what had he got in return? He had been criticized each time. " Archi started sobbing in excitement. Amar had said nothing. He was sitting. Kiran aunty felt frustrated. Still she said, "Everyone likes Amar except a few bad men. I am requesting you Amar, change your mind. Don't go."

"No aunty, actually I should stay where my job is. Instead of staying there, I travel twenty miles every day. Moreover, I will be transferred to a new place soon, Amar said."

"You can cancel the order of transfer. Your bosses know you very well. They won't deny you. The foxes of the village don't understand you. Forget about them. But think about the village people," Kiran aunty held Amar's hand. Her eyes were filled with tears. Amar stood up and went out to the yard. His three-year-old son asked, "Father when are we going there? Are we going by bus or by train?"

Amar said nothing. Kiran aunty went away rubbing her tears off. Amar came back and sat in the same place. He thought of visiting some people's house. He dropped the idea because if he visited someone's house it had to be one of those who loved him and there he had to face the same kind of requests. Therefore, he sat in the same place until dark. Amar had heard someone shouting and swearing on the road. The man was none other but Bholada. He was in an inebriated condition and walked with unsteady steps. He opened the gate and reached the yard. He shouted from the front yard, "Amar, are you home?" Amar stood up and replied, "Yes Bholada, come in." All the children of the house had gathered in the verandah. Bholada said,

"All of you should stay away from me. I am drunk. I am not a good man. Go away from here." The children got into the house. Bholada looked at Amar for some moment. His stained khaki dress made it obvious that he had straight forward come from Sharma motor garage. Bholada's condition told Amar that all the talking would be done by Bholada himself and he just had to be a patient listener. Generally, Bholada visited no one and attended no ceremonial function. "Amar, are you leaving tomorrow?" Bholada threw the first words. "You are a fool," he again started. "I am a drunkard. I always swear. But I am in control of myself now. If you don't like me please let me know. That Prasad, son of a brahmin has destroyed the village. He visits each house and instigates them against each other. When his brother was ill you helped him. You have established a school so that his brother gets a job. You have helped Renu in getting the job in a cooperative. But Prasad has bribed some corrupt officers and registered the job in his own name. After getting the job he has told Renu that you have been trying to give the job to your sister. He has created the misunderstanding between you and Renu's family. He brings sugar, rice, flour, etc from cooperatives and sells them in the black market. He has managed the officers by bribing. He instigates the people of the village against you. He tells Sujit to kill you so that his brother can get the job. That crooked fellow, he advises people to be honest, pure and be united. I am a drunkard; I have read up to eight standard. He is a matriculate. Yet, he can't pronounce a word properly. He pronounces 'Heart Weak' as 'Hard Weak'. His house is so dirty that even a drunkard like me hesitates to enter. He criticizes that you don't wear the scared thread. He considers himself superior because of that. I am a drunkard, I don't talk to you. But I keep an eye on everything. You have spent money in building the road. But what have they done? They have complained to the MLA that you have mishandled the finances allotted for the road. They should have urged the MLA for the improvement of the road instead they have complained against you. Amar, if you are bored tell me. I am drunk you know." When Amar's wife entered to offer betel nut, Bholada said to her, "You know dear, I have seen Amar growing up. He is very honest. He has grown-up in our lap. I drink nowadays, so I don't talk to him. I feel proud for he is a famous writer now. I do not read. But I have told everyone at my home to inform me if Amar's play is aired in the radio. I listen to his plays. I am a drunkard. You should not stay here. Amar, let me know who is against you. Chandraprasad is just a clerk in the police department. But his words are higher than his position. His aunty died of blood pressure but he has informed the police that his uncle had poisoned her. It has caused lots of harassment to the family. Now, he is after you. You advised his daughter to behave properly. But he has accused you of beating his daughter. I am warning you Amar, you cannot leave the village."

Bholada rose and went to the gate with unsteady steps. He shouted from there, "Amar, I may be a drunkard, yet my heart is pure." He kept on swearing on Chandraprasad as he passed through the road.

Amar couldn't sleep at night. He liked to help the poor people about whom he wrote in his novels, dramas and stories, etc. But in reality the people whom Amar had helped at some point of his life were all against him. They envied him. It was mainly because he spoke the truth directly without caring for anyone and secondly, Amar did not care for the caste system and removed the marks from the hypocrites of the society. Once, one worshipper of goddess Kali threatened Amar that he would harm Amar. Amar had told him to do whatever he could at the earliest. But Chandraprasad started spreading rumour among the village people against Amar. Amar loved to help people. He had never accepted anything in return from anyone. In these conditions when he had felt the wind blowing against him he was hurt. He had turned speechless. Seeing his condition Archi said, "That's why people go to cities. The village of your imagination is no more there. Let's go away from here. Outside this village the world is ready to welcome you. You are a bad person here. Let's go."

Amar rose from his bed without sleeping a bit. He checked his belongings. People had started coming to their home from early morning. But Amar had talked with no one. No one had tried to talk with Amar. What Amar feared most was infamy. Prasad, Chandraprasad, Rebatiballabh, Gajendra, Fulan, etc. had spread a lot of rumors against Amar. Rebatiballabh had falsely accused Amar of mishandling school funds. Amar's face dropped hearing the accusation. Amar had worked so much for the school. Prasad had created misunderstandings between Amar and Renu's family.

Amar was sitting at the railway station with bag and baggage. His nephews and other boys who had come to see them off were also sitting quietly. Amar's three-year-old son was playing in the platform. Bodheswar and Akanman had come almost running. Bodheswar was a daily labourer and Akanman sold betel nuts and bananas near the cinema hall. Bodheswar had said almost crying, "You have given me life by taking me to the hospital. Otherwise, I would have not lived till today. Amar, please don't go. You have done a lot for the village."

"Amar, you don't like calling you 'Gosai'. But I have observed from each and every side that you are perfect to be called as such." Saying this, Akanman held Amar's hand.

The whistle of the train was heard and everyone became alert. Amar's son said. "Father, the train has arrived. Let's go."

Akanman and Bodheswar were holding Amar's hand. Their eyes were filled with tears. Archi proceeded towards the compartment. The train stopped here for six minutes. Bodheswar and Akanman wanted to say something but could not express.

All of a sudden Amar had seen that a young lady and man were trying to board a sick man into the compartment. It was obvious that the man was very ill and they were poor. The lady was pulling the sick man while the man was trying to push him in. They had been trying without success. Amar proceeded towards them and helped. Bodheswar and Akanman also helped them. The sick man somehow got into the train. The train started moving with a whistle. It speeded up. Amar, Bodheswar and Akanman were looking at the train. The train was moving. Amar was standing on the platform....

Bloody Walk

We were lost in the crowd. Lots of people had gathered in that part of the town. The town could have been covered from top to bottom had the people gathered in the place been converted into a sheet of tin. We had proceeded towards Sivadol. There were people everywhere. I was visiting the Sivaratri Mela in Sivsagar for the first time. My elder brother said that Siva was the leader of the non-Aryans. Lord Siva was the very first communist. Some opportunist gods had feared that Siva could raise a rebellion with other exploited non-Aryans and could capture them. So, the leading gods had tactfully convinced Siva to join them and had made Siva puja prominent of all the pujas. Then onwards Siva had been prayed as god, the Lord. I had remembered all these and had told to Rupam and Parimal who were beside me. Mukunda and his wife Pratibha who were also with us had laughed at my story. Pratibha nabau had said, "You should not mock God." We all had laughed.

We were proceeding in a crowd. We had climbed the stairs and reached the yard. The crowd was pushing each other. In this crowd, I had felt very lonely. Thousands of people were surrounding me. Even Rupam was holding my hand. Yet, I had felt as if I was moving around in an uninhabited island. The crowd reminded me of the **Long March** under the leadership of **Mao Tse Tung.** People from various age groups had gathered here. Young girls could be seen in colorful attires. We were moving forward by making our way in the crowd. Once I had tried to punch a boy aside only to realize that it was a girl in the attire of a boy. I had hurriedly blended within the crowd otherwise, I would have been humiliated by the public. Rupam had noticed the incident. He had started to laugh. When I saw the foreheads of the young men smeared with red markings a strange sensation passed through my body. My residence was near a training institute. The minimum qualification for the trainees was graduation. But I was astounded when I had seen them standing in the queue for prayer holding earthen lamps and wood-apple leaves. They were all standing there for the fulfillment of their wishes. I was perplexed. A person who had passed MA was the final product of the society. He was the cream of the society. I didn't know how to react other than perplexed when I saw the final product of the society depending on insensible forces for the betterment of their lives. He had no difference with the illiterate Maheswar of our village. Both of them considered God to be responsible for their misfortunes. I felt nothing except pity for them. Poor educated young boys.

We were roving around the temporary stalls in the mela. We had stopped near a line of stalls selling things made of iron like dao, knife, sickle, saw, hoe, etc. In the front of their stalls there was a line of stalls selling clothes, toys, cutlery, etc. These stalls were stuffed with crowd. Rupam had uttered looking at the stalls, "Ashimda, no one will be able to imagine that famine may occur in our country if they see these stalls." Suddenly, I felt that fourteen-year-old Rupam had grown up. I had passed a smile and said, "These are all intoxications of marijuana and opium." He had asked, "What do you want to say?"

I had kept mum for some moment. I had thought of ways to express it easily to him and had said, "Rupam, let me tell you a story first. Suppose this Sivsagar town is a country. It has sovereignty and I am the king of the land. In every country there are people who sponsor the king. This species never does any hard work. Because of their intelligence they spend their lives happily depending on others. This species that includes me too have assembled fortune for generations to come. We are collecting the fruits of their toil and hard work. They are becoming poorer day-by-day. As the king I know that one day they will understand the truth and will start a rebellion against me. Then, there will be none to save me. So my responsibility is to distract them from the truth. As a result I will make them understand that an unknown invisible force is responsible for their misfortunes and hardships. I have to tell them that they will never be able to see or meet the force but will be able to feel its presence in every step of their lives. If their children die of hunger, I have to explain to the wailing parents that it is their destiny - consequence of their previous birth. God is punishing them for their misdeeds. Then they will leave everything in the hands of that unknown power. Suppose a child has a ripe mango in his hand. You have distracted him pointing towards the sky and snatched the mango from his hand. When he looks back, you say pointing upside, "That thing snatched your mango." He will start believing that some unknown force took away his fruit and you will keep on snatching the ripe mangoes. It is same in my case also. Intoxication is a trick to help me escape from the people whose fruits I am snatching away. An intoxicated man reveres even an earthworm. That is why the intoxication of marijuana and opium is greatest of all. I am snatching their fruits and they are praying to God. "God, please.......!" Isn't it intoxication? Saying this I looked at Rupam." He was listening to me attentively. I had no idea whether he had understood or not but after saying these I had felt good.

We were proceeding with the crowd. I was feeling good. Fourteen-year-old Rupam had seemed to me as my bosom friend. I was even avoiding my friends fearing lest should I need to send Rupam away. My friend Parimal had made fun of me because of this.

Although Parimal was just joking, his words hurt me. I had again said, "Rupam, just imagine for a moment, when they will know that Siva is not responsible for their condition. They are all sons of god and god never makes his son suffer. In that position, can you imagine what my condition will be? They will look at me and in a blink of an eye they will be chasing me with weapons in their hands. Just imagine the situation."

Both of us laughed.

After that we circled round the Siva temple and came down to the road though the south-west corner. There were thousands of people everywhere. My mind was wavering around and fancying things.

We had not moved further. Suddenly, I had seen a lump of flesh come rolling. In a mechanical choice he was shouting thrice in a second, "Hare Ram, Bom Bholanath. Hare Ram, Bom Bholanath." The man was proceeding towards the temple rolling. He was totally nude. Even the hairs of his body had fallen. It was because he was rolling. People giggled looking at him and changed their direction. Seeing the sight, I had started shivering. I had felt as if I were nude too. I had tried to cover myself with my hand. I could not look at other people. I had felt as if all were naked. All of them were nude. The man was rolling. I was standing among nude people. I was also nude. I had clutched Rupam's hand in fear.

With fear, I had stepped on the footpath. I had shouted like a mad dog in my mind. I saw this woman whenever I came to the transport station. She stood below the neon lights and put off the piece of cloth she was wearing on her waist. She was rubbing her sexual organ with that piece of cloth. She was having menstruation. The piece of cloth was in her hand. The people passing by were tittering. I felt as if the mad woman was trying to snatch the clothes from others. I had noticed Rupam. His eyes were filled with fear, anger and hatred. I had grown courageous.

We had started walking hurriedly. Hearing some noise we had looked back. A boy was running with a thud. His age could not be guessed looking at his face. A group of people were chasing him shouting. The boy had a packet in his hand. He tumbled down. He had got up and started running on the footpath again. He had passed in front of us. His feet might have been cut. The imprint of his bloody footsteps was visible on the footpath. People had gathered after sometime. They could have caught him.

My head started spinning. Both the rolling man and the mad woman were mocking us pointing at the vulgarity of our society. The hungry boy with the bloody feet gestured towards a bloody path lying in front of us. I had stared shivering. Everyone was shivering in my eyes - some were in fear of losing and some after losing.

CONCLUSION

Respected people!

You and I both have gone to the Sivaratri Mela. You too have witnessed the scenes that I mentioned. I too have seen who is crazy here? Of course, it's me. The impressions of the scenes are reacting very badly in my mind. Why not? I have passed MA seven years ago. During these years, I have prayed a thousand times to God for a job. I have even desired to offer puja if I succeeded. I have paid offerings to God as many as possible. Still I have not got a job. One day God had said to me that he was not responsible for all these. I don't know whether you will believe it or not. After that I know who is responsible for the situation. Now I want to ask you - do you know the culprits? Answer me.

There is no necessity to search for me; I am within you, roving around you. I am Ashim Dutta. I have passed MA and still unemployed. Come out of intoxication - you will know me. If you don't want others to hear you then whisper. I will listen. I will listen to your whispers also.

Glossary

Nabau: The term referring to the sister-in-law.

Dao: A large knife.

Compassion towards the Poor

A hiatus had been created at home regarding the girl. The question she asked put her parents into trouble and they felt embarrassed. They did not answer these questions, rather they were happy to escape from such tirade. But her modus operandi created laughter at home. Her family members rolled down after hearing her strange questions. But she did not laugh but she looked at the smiling face s of her family members. The way she kept on looking at them gave the impression that she was really worried regarding the smiling faces of her family members. Her question put her family members into an uncomfortable zone. Sometimes her father could not tolerate this and rebuked her mother, Aparna. Generally, every father liked her daughter more. That is why when she was born after her two elder brothers the joy of her father knew no bounds as he distributed sweets publicly and also forced the doctors and nurses to eat sweets. Likewise, he offered a note of five hundred rupees to the nurse who brought this ecstatic news to him and his reaction was like the ancient king on zamindars who behaved similarly on such occasions. Moreover, the attendants of other patients at the hospital were also offered sweets and tea. What amount did he spend? Maybe two thousand or three thousand. It was quite simple for DTO Paran Pujari. He desperately wanted a daughter after two sons. Now, he was least worried as God had given him a daughter. If this time too had there been a boy then he would have named him, Himanta. Now, there would be no more issues. Now, this same father came back home quite early from office, club and he did not also drink at home as the girl did not like the smell of alcohol. Even if he drank outside he did not fondle the girl immediately by taking her into his lap. He kept on pulling his leg from a distance, made her laugh or whenever she slept he played with her hands and touched her butter like cheeks and derived tremendous satisfaction.

Now, when Himana came towards him the father became extremely conscious as though the minister of the department had come.

He pretended to be serious. He opened a file without any specific reason and looked at it in order to avoid Himana's question. So, afraid was the father. She was just six or seven-years-old but precious enough to bother others and that is why the father blamed his wife for all this as he was terrified on occasions. Whenever he got opportunities in absence of Himana, he scolded his wife. Sometimes when the mother-in-law arrived at home she also rebuked the daughter–in-law when the girl annoyed the grandmother. Because of a plethora of reasons this small girl created danger at home. It was better to describe the environment before citing an example of the danger created by the girl. Because there were children in everyone's home, but everyone did not land in trouble because of his children. Then, how come the ambience that Himana did created problems for her family. Who had created such an environment? How is it that it had come to such a pass.

Aparna happened to be the eldest daughter of the head clerk of DTO office, Jadav Thakur. She was exquisitely beautiful. The newly arrived young professor kept on looking at the beautiful face of Aparna and it had become almost a routine. This had also given birth to jealousy the reason why the newly arrived DTO became impatient to marry Aparna when he first saw her at the resident of the head clerk. Then he was not reminded of his beloved, Alpona. He continued his love affair with Alpona for a period of seven years. In fact, he really continued his love affair. He proposed for Aparna to the head clerk, Jadav Thakur through other workers of the office. Jadav Thakur was surprised. It was beyond his comprehension that the DTO who was also a resident of Guwahati would really want to marry his daughter. Jadav Thakur who became the head clerk of the newly recognized district earlier worked as head assistant in the Deputy Commissioner's office. Jadav worked there and he had to travel almost 20 kms to reach his office from his village. He did not have a son. He had three daughters. After completing her graduation, Aparna was at home for a few years. The father kept on searching for a suitable groom. In many cases some people wanted to marry her. The younger ones were studying in college.

Thakur wanted her daughters to get married before his retirement. What more could a clerk desire in his life? On such occasions, DTO and a resident of Guwahati was really god's grace. It was like getting a wonderful feast which one could not expect. In spite of that Jadav Thakur was embarrassed on many grounds and his concerns were equally shared by Aparna.

But the marriage materialized.

It was almost twelve or thirteen years now. Aparna and Aparna's family members regarded the marriage as an incident. DTO Paran Pujari was also settled at Guwahati now after working in several districts of the state. It was very difficult now to turn him out of Guwahati.

Nobody could remove him from his present position, even a minister was also incapable of doing so against Pujari's wish. He had got three children. The elder son was almost twelve-years-old but still Aparna had not been able to settle down. As her husband had been constantly transferred from one place to another, Aparna had not been able to adjust and adopt. She had also been uprooted from his village and from the home of her honest father, who was the head clerk. But nobody had been able to transfer Aparna's mind. Nobody could do so. In the midst of such abundance Aparna felt lonely. This vast city – Guwahati appeared to her to be solitary. Aparna felt like a beggar in the midst of plenty. She felt thirsty even though she was soaked in water. This grandeur and this abundance, everything appeared to be distant to her. At this precise moment she was reminded of many lovers who wanted to marry her. She could have got everything with anyone of them. Nobody could refute Paran's reasoning, "Your father is like Bidur. Father got the job through a oral test and after showing the certificates. But what happened to me? How did I manage the job? I secured star marks in matriculation and stood first division in higher secondary examination. I also secured first class in M.Sc. I was at number thirteen in the merit list in the examination for the job. But I had to bribe eighteen lakh rupees in order to get the job of DTO. Please keep in mind the fact, then? Who shouldn't I take bribe?"

I had to get back my eighteen lakhs. Why shouldn't I take a bribe of forty lakh rupees? I had to pay in installments. I knew that because of these reasons my father–in–law did not visit our home.

Aparna could give the answer. That is why she was lonely. The sons were also like their father. They were studying in Don Bosco. Aparna made the best possible effort to teach them Assamese. But she failed in her attempts. Now, they could not read Assamese. They spoke in English with their father. But when Himana was born Aparna was determined to make her a real human being, not a machine. Sometimes she expressed concern regarding the fortune of her daughter. What would happen if the daughter also felt lonely like her mother in an otherwise crowded city. Only one consolation was there – that she would stand on her own feet. That is why Aparna had trained Himana in her own way since the day the daughter learned to speak. Aparna wanted that her daughter should not be dependent upon her husband. She started teaching her Assamese alphabets since an early age . She was sharp that is why she could easily grasp. Moreover the daughter objected against the idea of going to nursery school when she reached four years of age. It would be an exaggeration to tell that the girl could read comics at the age of four, could read magazines, could read newspapers. Like her father she read the newspaper spreading her legs and she also followed her grandmother. The scenery created entertainment for everybody. But an incident took place in the meantime. Himana could read the newspaper in full flow and then she would run to Aparna. If she did not find her mother there and discover that Aparna was in the bathroom, then Himana would run to his elder brothers. They denied in a straightforward manner as they could not understand Assamese. Hardly had she run to her father, at that moment the father would be talking to a few flatterers or be busy in some mathematical equations.

"———father what is meant by rape?"

At first father would not give importance to Himana's query but when the other people who were sitting along with the father laughed, then he would become aware of his daughter's query "Baby what did you ask?".

The flatterers keep on laughing and said, "ask her again."

What was meant by rape?, Again there was a sound of laughter. The person sitting near him thought he would encourage their humour . But the father was angry. Himana did not understand the logic behind her father's anger. He pointed at the first page of the newspaper in her hand and said, "look, what is rape?" Paran Pujari felt tremendously agitated. He looked at the news "A girl died because of the gang rape." After that he threw away the newspaper and goaded Himana to go to her mother and ask her the question. After the daughter went away, he scolded the people associated with the newspaper and also expressed his discontent with his wife. The flatterers agreed with him and told that the newspapers of Assam were full of news regarding rape, corruption, fund embezzlement and death. But many people did not know that occasionally the owners and reporters of newspaper also demanded money.

Wasn't this information suffice that the family members of Himana suffered because of such news? That is why Paran Pujari expressed his discontent as Aparna had registered her daughter's name in an Assamese school. Aparna kept on avoiding all those allegations because she was nurturing hope in her heart regarding Himana. She did not protest. Himana was good at studies, she was sharp.

It was an expensive school even though being an Assamese medium one. Himana was not required to sit on the mattress. Occasionally, the headmaster of the school halted the maruti car and said, "your daughter is really good in studies, she will definitely get first position." But Aparna did not want her daughter to study in such an expensive school with fifteen hundred rupees monthly fees. Rather she wanted her daughter to study in a village school where she would also learn to carry a bag full of rice. Aparna wanted her daughter to become a genuine human being. She would sit on a mat, would be soaked in dirt and mud. Aparna did not want her daughter to consume expensive foods like boiled eggs, butter toast , grapes, cashewnuts, rather she wanted her daughter to eat simple rice.

Aparna wanted her daughter to know people. She wanted her daughter to see the country. She would learn what was meant by a human being.

Aparna had the satisfaction of possessing Himana. Like Bitopan and Bimohan, she had not turned to be father's daughter, but she was her mother's own daughter, own Himana. At least till now. But if she turned out to be like her contemporaries then what would happen? Aparna was terrified to contemplate that Aparna had been able to retain her ownness, had compassion, honesty and integrity. Nobody could snatch away these qualities from her. She had turned out to be a genuine human being. That is why some times Bitopan and Bimohan appeared likes strangers to Aparna. Or they appeared to her as stepsons. She had lived for almost fourteen years with her husband but still he also appeared to her a stranger. Similarly, the two sons also evoked similar feelings. The older they grew; little was the possibility of knowing them.

Paran scolded Aparna. Actually he rebuked her using strong words. Aparna did not utter a single word. One club had organized a beauty and fashion show. The DTO Paran Pujari had given them an amount of rupees one thousand. But, DTO could not attend the show. Suddenly he had to accompany a minister somewhere. He was bound to go. That is why Aparna had to attend the show on behalf of her husband. But in the midst of all this Paran abused Aparna by calling her a typical village dweller, the daughter of a clerk, etc. He had also scolded because she had converted the daughter into a girl with narrow vision. Aparna did not want to attend such function and moreover her daughter would also want to accompany her mother. She would naturally accompany her mother but Aparna did not want to pollute her daughter's mind who was just above six years of age.

Aparna was able to sanitize her daughter's mind after making lots of sacrifice and that is why she took utmost care to excuse that she did not become contaminated. But Aparna was helpless in front of Paran Pujari. She had to go, She must go, She went.

The function was going on. Aparna and Himana were sitting on the first row of the hall.

The person sitting nearer to them was probably the minister and commissioner's wife. She was exposing her flesh because of the cloth she was wearing and seemed as though she would also participate in the fashion show. In order to avoid any possible conversation, Aparna was looking straightway to the show and she was also taking care of Himana who was too restless to sit in a particular place in a quiet manner. The female participants were wearing less clothes; they were also disposing off their remaining clothes one by one. They were exposing their breasts which were dancing on rhythm with the background music. They basically wanted to cash on their sex appeal, which they were adopting in doing. The audiences were thrilled to watch such bravo, such desperation and such pomade of nudity. They were shouting at the top of their voice, clapping, whistling and almost getting frenzied. Aparna felt like closing her eyes. Aparna felt like a woman without her attire as the female participants were displaying their semi-naked body which created enthusiasm and uproar among the audience. It was fortunate that all the lights were concentrated on the stage and the hall was dark. Aparna was shy of her own daughter Himana who just crossed six years of age. Aparna got a momentary relief as the daughter did not ask any question. But Aparna was already afraid of the possible questions that her daughter would ask later on. People like Poran patronized such functions in order to see such vulgar parade of shameless females. They gave hefty amount of fifty to sixty thousand rupees. If Poran was devoid of any urgent work, then he would have been there to witness the show. She looked at Himana obliquely. Himana's glittering eyes were fixed on stage. Suddenly she got up from her seat and went towards the stage. He threw away a few coins of five rupees at the semi-naked participants who were displaying their breasts. As there was a microphone it created the sound when the coins dropped on the ground. On every direction of the stage there was a microphone. The announcer hurriedly came carrying the microphone in her hand and she was also dressed like the participants.

He said in a self and artificial tone, “My affectionate sister what did you throw?”

‘I threw money,” Himana replied in a courageous and complete tone using the microphone that the announcer was carrying and the entire hall tuned out to be silent.

“Why did you throw money? Why did you do so?”

“My mother always says that we should be compassionate towards the poor,” Himana replied.

“Is it so? Where is the presence of any poor person here?”

“That girl, isn’t she poor?”

“Who told you that she is poor? Sweet baby how did you know her to be poor. Please answer.”

“Because they are not wearing clothes. All of them are wearing torn clothes. They are not properly attired. They are wearing torn clothes because they are poor. They do not have money to buy clothes. They are indeed poor and you too are.”

Definition of Love

I met the man thrice a day sitting on a sack. In front of him lay some furniture. By his side there was a wooden box where his customers sat. The frail man wore a clean pyjama and collared shirt. Though his clothes were not ironed yet it was clean. The man left his bicycle leaned on the walls of the closed shop and cleaned his business place. He kept his box in the right place, arranged the instruments and looked at the road with indifference rubbing tobacco on his palm. Right at this moment, I passed by. After getting down from the bus with the briefcase in my hand, I walked down the hundred meters distance on the footpath to the office, where I met him for the first time . The second time, I met him when I came out of the office for a cup of tea during the midday. The third time, I met him when I came back after having tea and finally when I came out of the office to catch the bus. I have later developed a friendly attitude towards the man whom I have barely known initially. A composed satisfied person.

"-----Mistry."

----"Ram Ram Sir," he saluted me raising the hand near his forehead. He did this in the middle of polishing shoes whenever I called him.

Though he was a cobbler, yet I have felt that he had some taste. I have never seen his beard except for a thin line of grey moustache under his nose. His hair was also grey. His frail body hid his age. After much pondering I had come to a conclusion that he must be somewhere around sixty-five years of age.

The man did not have much idea about my work, yet looking at my clothes and briefcase he had assumed me to be an officer. That is why whenever I called him Mistry he raised his hand to salute me. The smile that he possessed at that time was a smile of contentment. He looked very satisfied. I entered the zonal office of the newspaper in front of his eyes. He couldn't read the signboard written in Assamiya and English. Though he couldn't read, yet he spoke Assamiya very well. But he had a prominent nasal tone. I found him reading books whenever he was not working. The books that he read were of Hindi language and those coverless books he must have brought from the scrap vendors. I was not a writer. Though I was working in a newspaper office. yet my name had not been published anywhere. I think any good writer would have written a story or novel on this cobbler. It's because every human is a piece of novel. One day without any word, I sat on his box and had offered my shoes to him. He was taken aback by surprise. The tobacco he was rubbing had fallen from his hand. He had created such a strange noise as if I had made a great mistake. To make the situation comfortable I had started talking to him.

"Where do you live?"

"In Muzzafarpur, in Bihar – replied the Mistry rubbing the shoes with a piece of cloth."

"What is your name?"

"Ramprasad."

"For how long have you been in Assam?"

"I was born here sir; my father came here at the age of sixteen."

"Have you worked your whole life on footpath."

"No sir, there was a shop beside the hotel of that college." Immediately the scenes from thirty-five, thirty-six years ago came to my mind. When we were studying in the college a well-built person with grey moustache sat in the small concrete chamber. The room was filled with shoes and leather. The students from the college ordered to make new shoes of their selected design. The workers did not get time to raise their head from work and have a look at the students sitting on the bench in front of their shop and engage in frivolous talks. I felt as if an old photo album had been opened in front of my eyes. "— That shop did very good business, didn't it? What happened to it?"

"After father died the owner of the house had told us to leave the room. They later registered a case in our name. It took ten years to solve the case. I lost the case. A lot of money had been wasted. The police forced us to leave it."

"What about the house?"

"There is a wine shop now. Even the book stall has been closed down. It has also been converted to a liquor shop. Two wine shops sir. One among them is a pub too."

After my work was done, I stood up and offered him a five rupee note. Ramprasad denied taking the money.

"No, No sir."

"You have to take the money, saying this I immediately walked towards my office."

I spoke to him every time I crossed him, but sometimes when he was surrounded by a swarm of customers, I didn't talk to him. Nowadays, I didn't give Ramprasad to mend my shoes. It's because he didn't take money for the second time also. Whenever I called him he looked at my shoes saluting me. Nowadays, I polish my shoes myself. The students of the college put their feet on the box and he carefully rubs off the dirt.

Sometimes I sit with Ramprasad and talk to him. A red hue spreads on his face whenever I sit near him. On Assam bandh or any other strike days when I come to office in my own car, I find him standing on the gates of my office. Hurriedly he opens the gate and cleans my car with a piece of cloth that he brings. He is so neat and clean that he even cleans the piece of cloth that he uses for cleaning the car. I often go to talk to him if both of us don't have any work.

"Do you live around here?"

"I live near the crematorium sir."

"Do you have your own house here in Jorhat?"

"No sir, we live in a rented house. It's a long house which belongs to a person from my own province. Kanairam deals in tobacco."

"How many kids do you have?"

"Three sir. Two daughters and a son."

"Do they still live with you?"

"No sir. My daughter escaped. One lives in Gohpur and the other lives in Lakhimpur."

"And your son?"

"He too escaped with a girl. I have heard he lives in Guwahati now."

"What is your son and son–in-law?"

"They too are cobblers. Is it possible for a cobbler's kid to get something better than that?"

"You and your wife live in the house then."

"Is she old? Where does she belong to?"

"She is not old sir, he said shyly and she belongs to Tezpur."

"Your's is an arranged marriage or love marriage? Ramprasad looked down shyly and smiled."

"What is her name?"

"Kalawati, She is very neat and clean sir. She also tells me to be clean."

"Did you choose her for yourself or your parents did?"

"I met her in a marriage sir, his face had turned red in shyness."

"Your wife has a beautiful name. She must be very good."

"Sir, to be honest, it's only because of her that I have been able to earn my bread."

"You should have bought a house of your own."

" I do not need one sir. I have turned old – how many more days will I live?'

I often sat with Ramprasad. Not only Ramprasad, from my childhood days I developed friendship with so called lower class people like rickshaw pullers, cleaners, peons, watchman, etc. I liked them. They also liked me. These people were much more natural and kind than those so called polished or higher class people.

"Do you drink Ramprasad?"

"I did sir. I was an addict. Once I suffered stomach pain. One day she told me to take an oath not to drink again. I have not broken that oath yet. She has kept my blood clean."

"You love your wife very much, don't you? Hearing this he started smiling."

I often compared the love of the common poor people like Ramprasad with that of other couples. Some times Raju came to meet me in my office. She hastily entered my office, sat in front of me and started telling me the sad tales of her family life. Raju's husband was my good friend. He teached in a college. Their's was a love marriage. Raju was also a teacher. But their family life was very scalding. No one could assume that Girjananda was so suspicious towards Raju. I too wouldn't have known if she herself hadn't told me. He would not let her talk just for two minutes even with the male relatives of the family. Wasn't this an unnecessary doubt, an illness? Moreover, Girjananda was jealous also. Girjananda demanded all her money the day she got her salary. In comparison to her, my and Ramprasad's story was different. For the last twenty-five years I had been giving my salary to Ranjita. Ramprasad was also giving his daily income to Kalawati from the next day of their marriage. Ramprasad liked to tell this.

How much love existed between this poor couple? In this loveless country it's nice to see such a love-stricken couple. Sometimes, I think that there is no sexual urge in the love between Kalawati and Girjananda. Their one is lustless love. That is why their love has not worn out yet. Sometimes, I want to ask Ramprasad about their sexual life, yet I can't. Civil Servant Biman Hazarika's beautiful wife who works in a bank has divorced him. The accusation is that he has illicit relationship with various women. He has even established physical relations with the eighteen-year-old working maid of their house. After having such a beautiful and cultured wife why one indulges in illicit affair? It is possible only to those who draw an equal line between love and lust. People like Ramprasad and Kalawati didn't have such high modern ideas and that's why their love was still deep and warm. It's nice to see such love.

"Mistry!"

"Ram Ram Sir!"

"Why did you go home early yesterday?"

"Sir, I thought it might rain. Kalawati doesn't like me getting wet in the rain."

"Does your Kalawati think you to be a child that you may get unwell so easily?"

"She takes extreme care of me."

"You got a very good wife."

"She takes care of my diet also. According to her after working the whole day, I must take a bit of fish or meat or an egg in my dinner. I love to see her happy. I don't do anything that she doesn't like. In our place each and every couple quarrels--- some drink, some has illicit affair with other's husband or wife. But we never quarrel. the people of our community die early only because of drinking. I have not died. Rather, I have forsaken the habit of drinking."

I was surprised to see that whenever Ramprasad thought of Kalawati he looked very satisfied. Nowadays , he brought Kalawati's reference every time. One day suddenly and strangely Ramprasad had said that he couldn't pass the night without her. Even if he didn't get to see her, he had to be in the same house where Kalawati lived. This was very strange. If we think deep it seems to be a sign of madness. I have developed a desire to meet the woman called Kalawati. But I have not been able to voice it to Ramprasad.

"Ramprasad, doesn't Kalawati watch movies."

"No Sir, she doesn't like to watch movies. After our marriage, I forced her to watch one. On the other hand, I regularly watched movies. But since she doesn't watch, I have too dropped the habit. Movie is not more important than her sir."

That very Ramprasad had not come for many days. The wooden box which he kept with my permission in the verandah of my office was lying there. After three days, I had become restless. My condition had become like the young collegegoer who has not been able to meet his beloved for many days. I had inquired in many stalls where Ramprasad sat with his box.

"Do you know where Ramprasad has gone? "

"Sir, he might be ill. His wife doesn't let him come if he is ill."

"Sir, he is suffering from viral fever. One day I asked a thela puller who lived in the same neighborhood with Ramprasad."

"Nowadays, everyone is suffering from viral fever."

I had felt relieved when I heard that he was suffering from fever. These hard-working people like him don't care for illness much. The moment his fever goes down he will be here.

But no. Ramprasad remained absent for the whole week. I had started to suffer from a guilt feeling. We had been friends for the last two years, yet I didn't have the minimum courtesy to ask his well-being when he had fallen ill. I had decided to visit him after the office hours. It would not be difficult to identify his house. He lived in a two-room long house at the end of the crematorium. The tobacco dealer who was the owner of the house had increased the rent. Many had left but Ramprasad had not. Kalawati liked to live in the house. So, he had paid more.

To the east of the solitary crematorium there was a long house. A few naked children with flowing nose were playing in front of the house. Seeing a well-dressed person like me they had come to an abrupt halt and had started looking at me like a strange animal of the zoo.

"In which house Ramprasad mistry lives?"

"The cobbler?"

"Yes. A ten-twelve years old girl had pointed to the southern part of the long house."

The kids had again started playing the moment I had crossed them. I had landed on the small verandah of the house and stopped there. I had heard Ramprasad talking to someone inside the house in a hushed voice.

"Why are you worried so much? I will be fine. Everyone suffers from fever and they get well too. I have taken medicine. Your worry will not lessen my fever."

"Ramprasad, are you at home?" I called. After a few silent moments I called again.

"Ram, Ram Sir. I am home."

After a few seconds Ramprasad came out of the house putting on a red blanket. He offered me a chair and himself sat in the murha. His eyes were as red as chili.

"Are you suffering from fever? For how many days?"

"It has been eight days, Sir. They say it's "Viral fever."

"Have you taken medicines?"

"Yes Sir, I am regularly taking medicines."

"Have you visited a doctor?"

"Yes sir – saying this he started panting. I touched his forehead to get an idea of his fever. There must be hundred and one or two degrees fever till then."

"Have you eaten anything?"

"I don't like eating. But sir, Kalawati feels bad if I don't eat when I am ill. That's why I am eating forcefully."

"Right – you should not stop eating even if you are ill and you should drink sufficient water too. Kalawati has done the right thing."

“I am leaving now. I shall come tomorrow again. Do you have enough money to spend?”

“Yes sir I do have, Kalawati always tells me to save something to use during illness.”

“Where is your wife? I want to meet her. Call her here once. With reluctance Ramprasad stood up and went in. And In a hushed voice he said, “Let’s go, Sir is calling you. He wants to meet you once. Sir, from inside he shouted, do you remember the bomb blast in the train of Tezpur–Rangapara line – we were in that train.”

“Is it so?” I felt sad hearing Ramprasad’s words. I thought Kalawati must have lost her feet and it would be painful for her to come out. But Ramprasad had never told me this. Or is it that he didn’t like to discuss his beloved wife’s handicapped condition.

“Let’s go, Sir wants to meet you. Although he is in high position he is a very good man.”

“Leave it Ramprasad. I shall come later.”

“Wait Sir, we are coming.”

Ramprasad came out. He somehow stood near me and brought out a rectangular object under the blanket. I held it in my hand. A framed photograph. The remaining incense sticks were stuck in a corner of the photograph. A dry garland was hanging from the photograph. A large bordered saree covering the head with a big red marking on the forehead. A round faced bright eyed woman’s face could be seen in the photograph. The photograph was shaking in my hand, that means my hand was shaking.

Sir, before she died in hospital Kalawati said to me– I shall stay in this house even after my death. I shall talk to you – Ramprasad gazed towards the photograph of Kalawati in my hand and smiled.

“I always talk to her Sir. She lives here.”

Disabled Watchman

What a horrible sound! The men woke up. Even the infant sleeping beside its mother started crying. In the pin drop silence of the midnight hours what kind of noise was it?

Mahatma Gandhi was standing in a twelve feet tall pedestal in the corner of the crossroad. Stick in hand, watch hanging from the waist , spectacles in eyes and dhoti above the knee. In summer if it's not raining some people slept under this Gandhi. These were the people who spend their day in bus stations, railway stations, near hospitals and on roads begging. But they wake up before dawn. There is a reason behind it. They clear their bowels beside the road before people come out. To excrete they sit side by side or sit back to back.

A few days back a woman was lying dead in that place. An infant was found suckling over her breast. Looking at the infant no one would be able to guess his age. He was sucking his mother's breasts attentively. In satisfaction, his eyes remained half closed. Clever reporter Pranit Bhuyan, who had come out early in the morning with the camera to see the movement of flood saw the scene, clicked a few snaps and published it in the newspaper next morning. Below the picture he gave a caption, "A small example of thousands of people dying in hunger in the country."

The Parliament session was going on. The opposition party and dissident groups of the ruling party who were trying to put the government under pressure got hold of the newspaper and started shouting in the Parliament House as if they had won the world cup. They had started shouting slogans demanding the government to resign and the parliament to be adjourned. The government immediately ordered an investigation to find out whether the woman died in hunger or she had become the victim of rape or abortion. The report had to be submitted the very next day. So, starting from the IGP to the petty constable everyone got busy. Couldn't she find some other place to die than the Gandhi Maidan? After a few days of the incident, a young man was found dead in the same place. The dead man was a member of some communist party. The members of the house had turned it upside down by their protest. The government became angry. Is not there another place for all these incidents? While the situation was still hot one night at about 2 p.m. people had heard some noise. As they tried to find out the source of the noise, they saw two young men trying to rape a twelve-thirteen year old girl. One of these two young men was the son of the leader of the ruling party. The hue and cry started again. The girl gave a statement. The Chief Minister had lost patience and scolded the minister father of the miscreant boy. "Your son got no other place to rape? And look who is the girl; a servant! For your son, I have been penalized."

In this burning situation a new incident had occurred. There was a sound of yawning. While yawning, it was snapping its fingers in front of the open mouth as if one furlong fat iron man was yawning and snapping with iron fingers. At first people thought it to be a bolt from the blue. It's because the sky was clear and starry. There was not a single gleam of cloud in the sky. The hearts of the people sleeping under the Gandhi had started beating faster. In the local police station the bell of 2 p.m. had been rung a while earlier. The city woke up. From the microphones of the city warning was given, "Citizens, don't be frightened at the unknown sound." After sometime the government microphones had also started to sound the same warnings. The whole country had woken up. Fortunately, the parliament had been adjourned for an indefinite time. Otherwise the sound of the Parliament House would have been much stronger than this.

By then the newspapers had been printed. So, the news could not be found in newspapers. There was just small news in a corner of the newspaper called **Sankhadhwani.**

From the morning, everyone was talking the same thing as if they didn't have any other business. From the oldest to the youngest; from the beggar to the minister everyone was chanting the same thing. They all were talking about the yawning and snapping sound of the previous night. Some said it was the forecast of a comet; some said some vehicle might have landed from another planet; some said China was experimenting some new weapons; some said it's a war cry on the part of Pakistan or Bangladesh. But the government said that it's a combined trick of the opposition and some miscreants to bring down the present day popular government. Foreign powers were also involved in this for sure. The government, police, army all had become alert.

That night people who were eagerly waiting to know about the sound had fallen asleep. It's past two. Still there was no sound. What sound was it last night? Seeing the powerful preparation of the powerful government it had hidden itself in fear. Just a few minutes left to three. The birds would start chirping after sometime. At that moment somebody yawned breaking the silence of the night. Again somebody snapped fingers. Almost forty people were sleeping heavily under the statue of Gandhi. They had proved it wrong that one could not sleep without eating. People who had taken rich food and slept in air conditioned rooms in two feet thick pillow could not sleep that night. On the other hand, those who were sleeping under the sky on grass were sleeping so heavily. Once again hue and cry started in the city. Those who were sleeping in Gandhi Maidan had jumped up. They had started shouting first. Sounds of gun fire were heard. Police might have misfired. The government had appealed through the microphones - not to be instigated, afraid of or lose patience. The powerful government would find out the source of the sound very soon.

Next day when the news spread throughout the country through radio and newspaper, the country came to a halt. Peace committees were established in the city. Scientific Society, Study Society, etc were also formed. The Investigation Committee was also established. In every house people had gathered weapons. The army was called. The armed forces were told to protect the houses of MLAs, ministers and various high ranked government officers. The poor had started wishing if the night didn't fall. Others waited for the night. The government people felt relieved that now if one million people died in hunger daily, if a million women were raped, even if poison was adulterated; no one would think or shout about it. Therefore, the government felt thankful to the creator of that strange sound.

That night no one had slept in the city. Everyone was waiting for the sound. The beggars of the Gandhi Maidan had also not slept that night.

It's almost twelve at night. The sound was heard again. The sound of yawning and with it snapping of fingers. Hue and cry started everywhere.

A skeleton-like boy who was sitting in the Gandhi Maidan had discovered it. He jumped up and pointed towards the statue of Gandhi. Everyone looked at it spellbound. The concrete statute of Gandhi was yawning and snapping its finger is front of its open mouth. After that the statue started saying, "I earned freedom for you. That doesn't mean you will convert me into a watchman giving the stick in hand. Hungry people will die near my statue, you will rape a twelve-year-old near my statue, kill someone in front of me, discuss about the adulteration in front of me. How long should I guard all these. You find this place very congested don't you? Break my statue and throw it away somewhere, you will find space and I will also be saved. Ten more people of you will be able to sleep here. Is that Nathuram dead? Oh! There are millions of Nathurams in the country now. I cannot walk. So what is the point of making me watchman? You remove me from this place. I am requesting you all. You won't be able to do it alone. You are very weak. Since your number is more all of you remove me together. Do it because I am suffering.

Feeling of Love

"I am leaving Narayan.."

"You want to leave Kaiti?"

"Yes! But I want to tell you something."

"What is it Kaiti? Afzal Ahmed thought something looking at Narayan Basumatary."

"We shouldn't visit each other for a few days. These days are not good you know. No one thinks about others."

" It's true Kaiti. It has been a great problem. No one seems to care about others. Everybody is out to kill another."

"Those who once shared the same 'bidi' have turned each other's enemy. Ya Allah!"

"We are saved Kaiti, situation is not that bad in our place."

"These things are like forest fires. It spreads rapidly. But there is a difference you know."

"What is it Kaiti ?"

"Forest fires spread itself. But these fires are spread by people."

"You are right Wti."

"The government might say anything. But we know how much Bangladeshis are there. How many of them are there in our village?"

"They are there too?"

"Bunch of them. I keep on warning our people that someday they will displace us from our own lands."

"It has really been a great problem Kaiti."

"That's why I am saying we shouldn't visit each other for a few days and do not roam around much searching for the last cow or goat."

"That's true Kaiti."

"I am leaving then. How is daughter-in-law?"

"She is fine."

"Please, take care and be cautious."

After Afzal Ahmed left riding his bicycle, Narayan Basumatary thought deeply about the matter. They must have been brothers in some other birth. In this birth by mistake one was born in a Hindu family and the other was born in a Muslim family. But both the husband and wife were so kind. They first met each other while selling kettles in the market.

Later, they developed such an affinity towards each other that would surpass any sibling. When Kaiti's wife suffered from anemia my wife sent chicken, fish, etc to his house regularly. Whenever I reached his house with all these Kaiti scolded me saying, "Allah! Why should you bring all these? Your sister-in-law is taking medicine. She will be fine. How would we manage the things that the doctor has told her to eat? Is it possible for us to eat meat of pigeon or egg every day? I am satisfied that Allah has given me the chance to earn my wage." To divert Afzal from the topic Narayan asked, "Kaiti, there is a castrated goat in Master's house. Can't we buy that?"

"What's the cost?"

"The cost is rather high. They won't accept anything below twelve hundred rupees."

"If we buy at rupees twelve hundred, shouldn't we be selling at least at sixteen hundred? "

"Yes. "

"It is possible to get sixteen hundred rupees for that?"

"No, no, not at all. We may at the most get thirteen to fourteen hundred rupees for that."

"Let's see."

Such a kind man! What does it matter if he is a Muslim? Both of us are cheated by our own brothers. Now we are more than brothers to each other. The man was restless during the first childbirth of my daughter. He spent the whole day and night in hospital. In the morning when he heard the child cry, a pleasant smile ensued in his face. While leaving he gave the child a hundred rupee note. Later, I knew that on his way back he bought some fish on the ghat of Gangadhar river and made curry of that and brought it to hospital for my daughter. He was happy because he got a grandson. If only everyone on earth would have been like him then there would not have been any fight.

Soru pona described the events at home which he watched in T.V in Master's house. Houses burnt. People killed. People running to safer places with their belongings. His mother had forbade Soru pona to watch TV but he did not listen to her. Coming home, he provided every minute detail possible - how many people were taking shelter in schools and colleges. How many dead bodies had been recovered? In which place the police van had been torched. How many houses and villages had been torched?

"Soru pona, you need not describe all these things. Haven't your mother and I forbade you to watch all these things? Uncle Afzal also has the same opinion. They might be Muslims, but after all they are human too."

"Father, you may be thinking that only the Muslims have been killed. But lots of our Bodo people and people from other communities have also been killed. I don't know how many people are killed, but be it Bodo, non-bodo, Muslim each and every community has suffered."

"But you need not discuss these matters so much. It hurts to listen to all these. So, you better keep quiet. Oh god! What's happening?"

"You know mother, Sir says these Christian fathers are instigating people. "

"These foreigners are here for trade, trade of religion. What love will they have for human beings? You just keep quiet? Don't discuss these matters at home."

"Soru pona kept quite. His elder sister was married off. He had one elder and a younger sister at home who were yet to be married off. He had been in touch with his sister regularly. The situation was under control there."

"Soru pona, why don't you ask about Lily's well-being, said his mother."

"I have been calling her from the public booth. The problem has not spread to her place. Lily baiti has promised me to present a mobile phone in the Bathow puja this year. "

"You might have asked her for that. Her husband is just a teacher in a primary school. Why should you ask for such an expensive thing to her, his mother said."

"No no, I haven't asked for it. You can ask uncle Afzal. He was by my side when I called her that day. He told me to call her and paid the bill too. That day she told that she will gift me and Mai chana a mobile each."

"Lily might somehow manage to give you the phones. But how will you people manage to run it? Don't you and Mai chana remember that your fathers are petty businessman who sell cow, goat, etc. Moreover, we have not been able to do any business for the last fifteen days."

"We will arrange. Mai chana gives tuition. I work as labourer; I might get a rickshaw from the village panchayat. I have enlisted myself for that and will give a bribe of rupees five hundred later."

"Nowadays, even our own brother doesn't care much. During the Bathow puja, Afzal brought new clothes for Soru pona and all others. He uttered when complained, "Don't they call me uncle? You please keep quiet Narayan."

Narayan was sad these days. Even the market was closed. The days seemed to be the days of adversity. Why were people killing each other? The poor were killing the poor. Kaiti rightly said, "Narayan, poor never have any caste, nor any religion. Poor have just one identity. It is that he is poor." Kaiti had not visited his house for many days. Even he had forbidden Narayan to visit his house too. Kaiti was near everyone's heart in his family. He had heard of war but had never seen it. He now thought whenever there was war the conditions must have been like this.

When Soru pona heard about this his heart started trembling. He felt as if he had stepped in front of a cobra. His heart started beating like a drum of Bagrumba dance of Bathow puja – dhoom, dhoma, dhom. what will he do? What were they discussing about? He just couldn't believe his own ears. They were discussing about attacking uncle Afzal's village tonight. There were many Bangladeshis. Won't they harm uncle Afzal too?. Won't they burn his house too?

He could not eat anything during lunch. As if something had stuck in his throat. Those sentences which he heard in the shop had stuck in his throat. His heart started throbbing.

"Why haven't you eaten anything ?"

"Mother, my stomach is not well."

"You should not eat outside. Let me make you a mixture of water and thekera."

He drank the mixture instantly. He spent the later part of the day restlessly. With the setting sun his fear increased. As the darkness fell he couldn't wait anymore. He couldn't decide whether he would send his father to give the news or he himself would go and give them the news.

He took the old bicycle of his father and started peddling as fast as he could. He was peddling towards Nabam's village. He had to return immediately after telling uncle Afzal all those things. Nowaday's, everyone was overly cautious. Everyone kept some weapons near at hand.

He started panting as he reached uncle Afzal's verandah. One by one he called everyone. But when he found no reply he started knocking at the door.

"Who is there ?"

"It's me uncle. Please open the door."

"Isn't it Soru pona's voice? Saying this uncle Afzal came out to the verandah."

"Oh God! Why are you panting? Is everything all right."

"Come inside uncle. Soru pona went inside the house and closed the door."

"Uncle, there is a great problem."

"What is the problem my son? Why have you come here in these troubled days?"

"There is a great problem."He couldn't say any more as if the things that had stuck in his throat had increased.

"What has happened my son? Please tell me."

"Uncle, some people from our village are planning to attack your village. He looked around in fear as if someone else was listening to them."

" What will they do?"

"Don't shout uncle. They are planning to burn it."

"Ya Allah! How do you know?"

"I have heard it with my own ears."

"Where have you heard?"

"In the shop."

"Who have said like this?"

" Those boys were discussing, uncle. But uncle no one in my house knows that I have come here. I should be going now. He was about to go out when uncle Afzal had caught hold of his hand and said, "You can't go alone. I am coming with you."

"No uncle. You needn't come with me."

"Why? asked his aunty."

"It's not safe to go out."

"Still, I will not allow you to go alone."

"Uncle you do not worry. I will manage. He opened the door and went out in the darkness."

Afzal Ahmed reflected what he should do. Taking the lamp in hand he visited every house. He warned them and told them to be cautious. Although some men were guarding the village, yet he had told them to take some more men with them. That night no one could sleep well. From the other village some people had come to attack the Nabam village. But when they came to know from their sources that people were guarding the Nabam's village they returned. That night no one in Narayan Basumatary's house too could sleep. Where had the boy gone? His father had repeatedly advised him not to go out of the house. "No one is enemy here. We have never seen Bangladeshis in our place. Why should you go to burn the houses?" In anxiety he started to scold his mother.

"Both of us are at home, aren't we ?"

"But it's the prime duty of the mothers to know about the whereabouts of their children. In these troubled days he has not returned home till midnight hours."

"Why are you scolding the boy who is not at home?"

"You may not be concerned for him. Madness has ensued over these boys. They are just out to kill another. They have demanded that the foreigners should be sent back. The government will do their job and fulfil their demand. Don't they understand this much."

"Why are you shouting so much at this hour of the night? Our son has grown up now. He might be with some of his friends. Bakhar, his friend is also not at home since evening."

"He may land in some trouble. These young lads! Neither do they study, nor do they work. They just know only one thing and that is agitation. Their motive is different. They seem hypocritical."

"Please keep quiet. Bakhar is also not at home. But do you hear any noise like ours in Bakhar's house too? Why are you shouting so much in this late hour of the night?"

Tears rolled down from uncle Afzal's eyes when Soru pona left his home. "This small boy has come to our home at this hour in these troubled days.

He is so concerned about us. They don't differentiate between Hindus and Muslims. This small boy has brought tears to my old eyes."

"I have a doubt."

"What is it?"

"Don't get angry."

"Let me know first."

"These days are not good."

"That's true."

"No one is reliable nowadays."

"So what?"

"May be....."

"What do you want to say?"

"Leave it. Go to sleep."

" What do you have in mind? Tell me."

"May be he had been sent as a spy.— What! What did you say? Allah! How could you think like that?"

" I am not thinking like that. I just have a doubt.........."

"Just for a moment, let's think you are correct. But don't you have the common sense to think that a spy would never disclose their plans or internal matters. Ya Allah!"

"That is also true. "

"It is rightly said that no one can understand a woman's mind. When you suffered from pneumonia did not Narayan sent various nourishing items for you?"

"I was just giving vent to my doubts, why do you get so angry?"

"Why shouldn't I be angry?"

"Relax now and go to sleep. It's almost morning. Nothing will happen now."

Although Fazal Ahmed went to sleep he remained cautious. His elder son's family was not here. The second son was living separately. Mai chana and Rahmat were living with them. If there happened to be any noise they would run to the forest through the back door. Just before dawn, Fazal Ahmed woke up hearing some noise outside. Why there is so much of noise? Where has everyone gone? Have they come to attack in these early hours of the morning? He went out to the road. Everyone was looking anxiously at the road.

"Hey Kermat, What has happened? Where are you going?"

"Kaiti, I have heard that a spy has been caught."

Fazal Ahmed started running. After running for sometime he had seen a gathering under the mango tree. "What might have happened there?" he questioned himself. He speeded up. He heard the clatter rising. He understood nothing. He proceeded pushing the people of the crowd aside. Some boys were kicking on a dead body of a young boy .The head of the dead body was broken. Fazal Ahmed moved forward to look at the face of the dead boy. Suddenly a wail came out from the deepest corner of his heart. The noise came to a halt. Fazal Ahmed kept on shouting. No one understood what he was babbling. Senseless, he fell near the dead body. Some people took him away and started sprinkling water on his face. People gathered there had decided to take him home and call in a doctor. The crowd was puzzled to see the old man crying for a spy. After much pondering over the matter they had come to a conclusion that since the boy often came to Afzal's house he must have some love relation with Mai chana. That is why there was hue and cry in the family at his death.

"Who is that boy ?"

"I don't have any idea. I have heard he belongs to Napamua village."

"Didn't the people of that village want to burn our village last night."

Suddenly Fazal Ahmed regained sense and started to shout, "Who has killed that angel? He came to warn us that some people wanted to burn our village. Those irreligious people have killed him on his way back home, Ya Allah! Please forgive me for my mistake." He went out of the house.

"Who has killed him? What shall I tell now to my brother Narayan? He had become senseless again. The people gathered in the yard stood stunned.

Gopal's Steps

Gopal had opened the book he brought from his classmate, Papu. His father shouted from his bed. Bring some consecrate water from **Gossain**. I have not been able to sleep even for a second last night because of the gripping of the stomach. His father's words had made Gopal angry. He had to return the book today. But he could not write the lesson. Last night the oil of the lamp was finished as he started writing. He went to the kitchen to write in the light of the clay oven. He felt dejected when he saw no fire in the oven too. He asked his mother, "Mother, haven't you cooked rice today?"

"We don't have a single rice grain in the house. Is it possible to cook without it?" His mother said clenching her teeth in anger.

"I have been suffering for the last four days; my stomach is aching so much. How would I manage rice grains for you?" the father said groaning.

"No one is talking to you. Don't try to quarrel. Why wouldn't you be ill? You drink so much. You are responsible for your illness."

"Don't think I am happy drinking? Work for a whole day in the hot sun - only then you will understand why I drink."

"Now, who is suffering?"

Without paying much heed to his parent's argument, Gopal put on his buttonless blue shirt. He put out two pins from the pocket and had sewn the two ends of the shirt. He had asked for the pins from his teacher. His teacher also scolded him why he did not attend school regularly. If he went to school regularly he would be able to sit for the scholarship examination. No one had got scholarship from the school for many years. He had a bright chance if he studied regularly. But he didn't have books, neither copy nor pen. The teacher had given him a pen and arranged for a few books. He brought from Papu the books he didn't have and wrote down the lesson.

"Gopal, hurry up! There is no use of studying. His father shouted again. Send a coin and some betel and betel-nut in his hand for the **Gossain**."

"We don't have a coin in our home. Don't just give orders."

"Don't you have a coin in your hand?"

"Wherefrom should I find a coin? Moreover, coins don't lay eggs."

"Will the consecration be of any use without offering a coin? Oh God!

Wrapping the betel-nut and leaves in a banana leaf and holding a bamboo tube in another hand Gopal started for **Gossain**'s house. He had to walk a mile. Again, he had to go to school after coming back. He was thinking of returning the book then. Gopal didn't like to go to **Gossain**'s house. He had to sit on the ground there. They allowed neither to stand nor there was any arrangement to sit on. Once he sat on the chair. The wife of the **Gossain** started shouting as soon as she saw him. "How do you dare to do this? Even your father doesn't have the courage to do it. Is this what you learn in school? Don't you know how to respect elders?" At first Gopal had not been able to make out why she was shouting . The moment he understood, he stood up blushing.

Lots of people had gathered in **Gossain**'s house for consecrated water. He had met lots of school going children while returning home. He speeded up. The **Gossain** warned him that if a drop spilled, the water would not be efficacious. When he handed over the bamboo tube to his mother, his mother asked him if the **Gossain** had given any instructions. He had replied hurriedly, "The **Gossain** asked if we don't have a coin to offer him." His mother kept quiet. He got ready to go to school. He hurriedly took a dip into the pond and finished his bath. He knew it was written in books that one should not dip in the pond for bath - since other members of the house bathed like that he also did. His four siblings were searching for fruits under the Bakul tree. His elder brother got ready to go to work in the brahmin's field.

"Where are you going so hastily? Mother asked."

"Going to school. I have to return a book to Papu. Teacher also scolds if I don't go to school."

"You are going to school! What will you eat? There is nothing in the house to cook."

"I will go without eating anything."

"Don't go to school hungry. Do you remember one day you vomited in school because you were hungry? Don't go to school. There is no use of studying."

Gopal didn't pay any heed to his mother. He had brought out some half-ripped banana peels one using his nail and started chewing. He didn't mind the taste of the banana. After eating the banana he drank some water from the pitcher, took his books and started for school.

"Hey Gopal, come here." He proceeded towards the teacher with hesitating steps. "How many times have I told you not to miss school? What do you do at home? Do you go to work? One day I told your father too. If you have been a bit attentive regarding your studies and constant in school, you would have got the scholarship. We are hoping on you. In the schools of the town, students get scholarship in hoards. Why won't they get? Their parents always take care of them. Don't allow them to miss school." "In our village, you know Rahman," he said looking at his colleague, Rahman, "In our village students miss school to look after their siblings. Why haven't you come to school these days?"

"Father is ill."

"So? What did you do if your father is ill?"

"Mother is busy taking care of father. Kakaideu goes to work in the brahmin's field. I look after the siblings."

"Oh! You are babysitting. How many brothers and sisters do you have?"

"Four."

"Four! After you..............! You know Rahman, our Gopal has four brothers and sisters younger than him. Our villagers don't have the land for rice cultivation, therefore, they do the human cultivation properly. This is the best cultivation in our country. Go to your place."

Gopal went to his own place. He couldn't say no to babysitting. Otherwise, his mother would beat him like anything. Today, he had come to school defying his mother's order of babysitting. He was anxious about the punishment that he had to face after going home.

Gopal's stomach was paining. The banana was not ripe properly. He had drunk cold water with that. He felt very hungry when he came to school without eating. At that time he had a sensation as if a snake was rolling inside his stomach. Is hunger like a snake? The snake tried to come out if it didn't get feed. One day his elder brother, Bor Pona said, "You know Gopal, while working I feel so hungry. It is better to be ill than to be hungry." He also thought the same. It is better to be ill than to be hungry. When Patoli, Hema and others cried in hunger, their mother slapped them. They kept quiet after that. As if it's better to get beaten than to be hungry. Hunger receded as soon as they got beaten.

Gopal slammed the books and ran to the jungle at the back of their house. His stomach was aching. For the last two days he had not cleaned his bowl. He somehow sat behind the bush and felt relieved. After clearing his bowel his pain was gone. Every day he thought of doing a latrine. It was written in General Knowledge books that one should not do it in the open. One day he started to build his own latrine. But his mother severely scolded him.

The moment he entered home his mother clutched his hand and said, "Didn't I tell you not to go to school today? Why didn't you oblige?"

"So what? I have not told you to give me anything to eat. Gopal had said."

"There was nothing in the house to eat. You at least could have looked after the children staying home. One of them has injured his head, another was about to fall in the pond quarreling with one another."

"You have produced those children. It's your duty to look after them."

"What! You son of a bitch. Are these things taught in your school."

The woman grabbed Gopal's hair, took a stick and started beating him severely. Gopal started howling. Hearing his cries, his brothers and sisters came out of the house. Hema had a cut mark on his forehead. Singora's calves were full with marks of beating. Gopal went to bed crying. After sometime he stopped crying. They could not light a lamp because of lack of oil. So he had thought of writing the essay in daylight that his teacher had given. The teacher had told to write an essay on Mahatma Gandhi as homework. He was told to submit it tomorrow. He did not want to get up from his bed. In the yard outside mother was working. She was scolding at the same time, "He has been working at the brahmin's field, yet has not brought anything home. Not even a basket of rice grain. He will be paid after harvesting." On the other hand, the father was groaning. The consecrated water had not shown any effect. Although he ran from **Gossain**'s house, yet he did not allow spilling a single drop of water. Gopal's stomach started to ache again. He would not be able to write the essay today also. The teacher would scold again. In the morning, he might again have to go to **Gossain**'s house to bring consecrated water."

Gopal had not taken rice at night too. He had no idea if there was something to eat. Hema asked him to eat. But he did not get up as his stomach was paining. He had not been able to sleep from midnight. He was waiting for the morning. He would write an essay on Mahatma Gandhi. He arranged the facts in mind. The most famous work of

Mahatma Gandhi's life was that he brought India freedom. We are a free nation now.

In the morning, he sat to write the essay. His mother said, "No need to study. Go to Shankar's aunt's house." Gopal had stayed motionless. Yesterday's incident was still alive in his mind. He couldn't deny. Not at least today. On the other hand, his teacher would scold him if he didn't write the essay. He would be hurt. He had scribbled inattentively a few lines - Mahatma Gandhi had brought us freedom through movement. We have become very poor. We don't have rice to eat... He asked his mother why he needed to go. Mother had said, "Tell Khanikar's aunty that our father is ill. Mother has told you to give two baskets of rice grain." Gopal started to think. He had to travel six miles and had to carry the grains in a sack on his back.

He hurriedly sat to write. He tore a page from the copy and wrote:

"Respected Sir,

Our father is very ill. We have not been able to eat for the last so many days. I have tried to write the essay. Today, mother has told me to go to aunt's house to bring rice grains. She will beat me severely if I don't go. Please accept my leave. I shall show you the essay tomorrow.

Yours sincerely,

Gopal."

He hurriedly folded the letter and ran to Papu's house. He gave the letter to Papu. His mother had said. "Hurry up Gopal. Sun is getting hotter. I will ask **Gossain** today. If he agrees you have to stay in his house from tomorrow." Listening to the last sentence Gopal's head started spinning. An ugly cruel picture of **Gossain**'s house started revolving in front of his eyes. When would he write an essay on Mahatma Gandhi? He had to show it to the teacher!

Suddenly his little head was filled with anger for Mahatma Gandhi. He had turned very angry. Holding an old sack he went out angrily. He walked in such a way as if he had gone out to meet his greatest enemy, Mahatma Gandhi. His feet were very small. Otherwise, the earth would have shaken with his steps.

Glossary

Gossain: A respected person occupying a place of dignity in Sattra, a place of religious and cultural ritual of the Assamese people.

Bakul: A kind of plant which blooms in summer.

Kakaideu:A term of addressing elder brother in Assamese society.

The House of the Dead

Bili got up from bed as soon as she noticed that Narayan somehow managed to embrace sleep. All the three boys and girls started moving around the house. Two of them were under the hog plum tree. One of them was standing below the marmelos tree. Coming out, Bili noticed that Rajen was looking straight up to count the numbers of the marmelos hanging in the tree. Those were raw marmelos. Bili filled up the earthen pitcher lying in the bamboo grove as usual. When one is hungry one eats something, but none of them had eaten anything at all.

Except Rajen, the second son of the family, all others shouted noisily at the time of hunger. Rajen resembled his father. He spoke less, and thought more. He would take many bowlfuls of cold water when he felt hungry and never shouted noisily like his elder or younger brothers. That was why he was dearer to his father than anyone else.

Nothing was left in the bamboo grove besides the bamboo stools. Some fire pieces of bamboos were still attached to them. All the bamboos were sold out. Bamboo-wood, cows and sheep - nothing was there in their household. Everything was sold out and exhausted. The man did not rise up from his bed. Injections and vaccines of different varieties were pushed into his veins, all forms of worship were done with utmost devotion. All the doctors diagnosed the patient. They took away hundreds of rupees as their fees - but the patient did not recover at all. One was desirous of taking away the eldest son of the family to put him to work in exchange of money. But nobody wanted to send the eldest boy to work, leaving his school and studies. Runu opened a school in the library. He was promoted to third standard in that school. Runu informed that the boy had been good at studies. He managed to get the first rank there.

Bili had been disturbed in her sleep for a week or so. She was a constant companion to the man. There was no oil in the lantern. It became totally dark. In the evening, she collected a heap of debris and lit fire to it to drive away the mosquitoes from the smoke thus generated. They would make their presence felt once more after a while.

Brushing her teeth with a tiny branch of an evergreen flower tree, Bili thought as to where to go that day for begging alms. There was none in the village who would offer help to that family. Almost all the villagers were having a tough time. A few of those who had the means to help others were found to be poor at heart and were not merciful to others. Bili had a dip in the small pond and stayed there. She dragged her 'chadar" (a kind of garment used by females in Assam) and rolled it, and at the same time she had a close look at the pond side. Nobody was there; she inspected her mammary glands which seemed to wither away like a dried piece of white 'dhatura' flower. Even a few days ago, Makhan the shopkeeper looked at her very closely whenever she would pass by his shop. He would tease and utter a few words about her. She had never paid attention to all these. The man was perverted by nature. He teased and taunted the girls and women whenever he would get an opportunity and sometimes would touch their bodies also. He had his own young sons and daughters at home. He had his own wife as well. All of a sudden Bili felt free in her mind when she was examining her milk glands. Not too many people could be found standing beside his shop in the afternoon. Why should the boys not cry at all? Was she feeling less hungry than them? How much could she drink water? Sometimes water would make its way to the mouth from her belly which tasted bitter as if it came from her spleen. The sons would sometimes say,"Oh mother, I feel my mouth tastes somewhat bitter, please give me something to eat." Was it so easy to supply the edibles the moment they wanted, what was really left to be given to them?

Narayan did not have that much of land and property. He was separated two years after his marriage. He could get only that plot of land on which there stood a house. The plot of lands were divided among the six brothers. He earned his livelihood as a daily labourer. Makhan, the shop- keeper would give items on credit if Narayan felt sick and could not go to work. He would like her to get more. He would weigh things on one hand and would speak on the other when no one was around."Narayan is very lucky indeed to get a person like you. You could have been more powerful than the wife of an officer in the town, had you been born in a wealthy family. Why upon earth did you come to this family at all? I wish I could see you earlier, then I would...." The situation would not have been such had her father been fit to go to work as a daily labourer. The man had swollen like a small goroi fish floating dead on the water. The body was wet. The legs had swollen like the stem of a big-sized banana tree. He could not void urine. Initially, drops of blood could be found in the urine. Someone told about the effect of evil eyes on the man and he used an amulet . Holy water was put into it, but he was not cured of his illness. His face also swelled like a rotten mango floating on water. The eyes shrank. The doctors declared it as symptoms of urinary disease. They advised the family to arrange to shift him to Dibrugarh, but how could Bili manage to shift him even though the doctors advised so? There was no one to bury the dead on one hand, who would provide the sandalwood sticks for him on the other? No treatment was going on at that moment. The man seemed to swell day-by-day.

Adjusting the wick, Bili thought what she could give the boys to eat. Last night also they had no rice. One of the elder brothers of Narayan sometimes visited to enquire about the condition of the family. The man would go to the chowk-market carrying a basketful of vegetables. Sometimes he entered into the house during his return. He would give away two bowlful of rice from his own family provision. He would also offer one or two stale vegetables to the family which he could not sell in the market. They could manage to eat rice till yesterday which was provided to them just the day before and their bellies remained half-filled. It was boiled rice with unclean water. The man also had multiple children in his family. He would not allow his wife to abort them opining that they had been gifted by God. But his wife got herself operated upon without disclosing the news as per the advice of the nurse, Mina. Otherwise the number of children would have been more in their family! Narayan said, "People fall sick when they do so. None should intervene in the design of God." But he fell sick instead without being operated upon. The men folk were really greedy. While his body had swollen like a sumo wrestler, he would put his hand on her breasts. She would put it away. He made a snoring sound, as sick as he was - but he was still greedy.

She had been feeling sorry for the man for the last three days or so. She was sure that her husband would not live long, she would boil the dusty remains of the raw 'pithas' (a kind of Assamese dish) and would offer them to the man in the mornings and the evenings - but he could not eat them.

The doctor advised him to take as much water as he could. But the man apprehended more swelling to his body and he dared not take too much water. Another problem arose when he took water as he could not rise up to avoid urine. He felt dizzy when he had to walk with support here and there. Twice he urinated on the bed. He could not tell it - he could only tell when a pungent smell spread across the room. Bili boiled the raw pithas given to Narayan by the newly married wife of Narayan's brother. Three of her sons swallowed them immediately. They were happy to find their father had not devoured them - they exhausted the 'pithas'. Bili did not put something aside for herself - she thought she would eat the uneaten remains of her husband. But nothing was left out. She drank two glasses of water. The glass was made of aluminum. Rajen said to his elder brother, "Got it, brother, we'd have to pick two wood apples today. They will be tasty once they are burnt in the fire." Hearing Rajen's proposal, all the three of them rushed to the wood-apple tree. Does it really take so long for the wood apples to get ripened? Rajen was a seven-years-old boy? His elder brother was nine years and their youngest brother, Pravin, was only five-years-old. Hearing the proposal, Mohan started pelting stones at the hanging fruits. Their mother came from inside and shouted, "The hungry devils, what makes you pit stones at the raw wood-apples! Would you love to die with head injuries? You fools will die in this process and make me die too." Saying so, Bili drew out a playing card sized mirror and looked at her face. She rubbed her fingers on a small piece of paper which contained vermillion and applied that in between the splitted hair of her forehead. But the red color was not visible on her forehead as there was no trace of vermillion powder on the paper. On the whole, she did that as part of her daily habit.

"I feel terribly hungry, mother - a brunt wood apple will stuff the belly," Rajen cried. "Did you eat the 'pithas' to increase the intensity of your hunger?" Saying so, Bili opened up the lids of a few tin cans. The other day, the elder one offered a few bakery (naan) biscuits while he entered on his way home from the market. Bili immediately snatched them and put them in one of the tin cans. If Narayan would refuse to eat the 'pitha', then these biscuits might be dipped in water to make them soft and could be given to him - he might eat. Or might not also. She opened up all the cans but found them nowhere. Those monkeys might have found them while searching and had eaten them. Not finding in the cans, Bili even went to search them under the bed. But they were nowhere to be found.

"What have you been searching for so long?" Bili did not give a reply to the question asked by Narayan and kept looking around

"Oh God, this woman never replies to a query. Your mouth is short of words these days. I am not fit to talk to as I am sick. God has kept me half dead." Saying so, Narayan was offering hiccups whenever he spoke a word or two these days. Sometimes it would seem that he might breathe his last. It lessened only when his chest was massaged on and the throat drenched with a little bit of water. Without speaking a word, Bili brought some water in the bronze glass and put it near the mouth of her husband. Using her right hand, she massaged his chest also. The hiccup subsided after a while and Narayan put his wet and swollen hand across Bili's neck and dragged her and said," 1 am not going to live for long. I could not have a sleep all these days thinking about your condition after my death. My eyelashes did not meet with one another", Narayan started crying. Though Bili did not utter a single word from her mouth, tears rolled down from her eyes through the dry cheeks. She immediately left the place. She shut the back door as she looked at the bamboo grove. 'Penpa', a trombone type musical instrument made of the horns of the buffalo could be heard from somewhere. She should not have remembered about Maghi even though the 'penpa' was being blown off. But she remembered. Maghi wanted to elope with her when she was engaged with Narayan. Her condition would have been different had she eloped with him. Maghi's cultivation had grown by leaps and bounds on the paddy fields of the village. He also erected a pucca RCC building. One incident suddenly crossed her mind which should not have come then. On the day of marriage of Sarumai and on the day of the Bhaona (a performance of an one-act play on the premises of the place of worship) Maghi made her feel on top of the world which she did not get even for once from that man for a decade. Perhaps she had been suffering then because of the sin she had committed before her marriage. Would he die as he had said so?

"Mother, what shall we have this afternoon?" Mohan asked biting a ripen hog-plum.

Bili went inside after telling to eat her head. There were no biscuits either. She could not think what she would give to the man. Even her belly was fully empty. People were not found in Makhan's shop in the afternoon. Makhan would not raise his head to see her even if she stood by him in the afternoon. His hands rose automatically to her dried breast as she thought in that way. Her hands touched her mammary gland which was dangling as a pair of burnt aubergines, she felt cold. They were like the withered away 'Dhatura' flowers.

The two elders who were a little well off did not take care of them. Although they took information about them but they could not offer things too much. Bili could not even think which house she would go to ask for a handful of rice so that she could boil them and offer them without draining off the water. There was none in her neighborhood to stretch out her hands for begging alms. People from her neighborhood would ask the moment they saw Bili or the three boys "Have you decided to go out somewhere?" They would not even ask about the necessity of going out. What would happen to them if Narayan would die one day? But then, what was the difference of his being dead or alive! One could hardly find people in and around Makhan's shop in the afternoon.

What if no men were there, although she was the only person standing before his face, but Makhan would not raise his head from his book. If he had found Bili alone a few months back, he would have pressed or bitten her like a sugarcane-juice vending machine. Then she would not come alone at that time. But at present he would not raise his head even if she would come alone.

After sometime, Makhan raised his head and said, "you have stayed here long enough. What happened?"

"I wanted to have a few items."

"Have you brought money with you?" .

Bili did not say anything. Makhan told her that previous credits had not been cleared. Credits had made him a bankrupt. He said, "I can't always give items on credit."

"I do not want anymore. But today, I wanted to have something."

"No, No. Don't touch them. I did not ask for money as your husband had been ill. The shop where I would purchase goods from, had also asked me to clear all previous credits. So, I had been looking for the credit amount from house to house. So, I would not give you. Go elsewhere and have items on credit." Makhan concluded his calculations in his book and closed it. He went out. He stood on the verandah and looked at people on the road. Once he went to the backyard of his shop. After standing for a moment before the shop, Bili also went backyards. Makhan was adjusting the soil around his aubergines plant with a spade. She stood at his back and demanded," Even if others don't, please give me a few bakery biscuits for some days and a little kerosene oil. I'll give you money after a few days."

"Don't trouble anybody in that way. The amount of oil that I get, is not enough to provide to the card-holders moreover, I have earned a bad name as a black marketeer. Whenever the supply is available, bring in money and take as much as you can. Don't demand right now", as he said so, he raised his head and saw Patali, the wife of Golap, standing before his shop. He smiled to see her. Patali also wore a wicked smile. Avoiding the presence of Bili, Makhan started teasing Patali. Bili understood that Patali had come to Makhan's shop at midday when none would be available. The 'Chadar' that she wore on top was slipping. One part of her breast became open. She also carried a bottle of kerosene in her hand. Bili came out from there to leave them free. Coming on the road, Bili thought where to get her kerosene from. How could she keep burning the dried leaves and take care of her husband also? Which house of her elders she would pay visit to - she put her strides in a confused frame of mind.

It was evening then and Bili's elder sister, Makhan must have gone out. Makhan had a bald- headed son of seven or eight-years-old. Though her house stood at a distance of four miles, Bili heard that her husband had died of cancer, but Bili could not pay visit to Makhan's house to get the information for a month or so. She could not leave the sick man at home and at the same time she had nothing to carry to the house of the dead. So, she could not go. Makhan had gone out accompanying her son. She brought kerosene from the house of the eldest brother measuring the length of four fingers in her bottle. She lit the lamp with that being sad; Makhan said that Bili did not visit her brother-in-law's house even though she knew that her sister's husband had been laid up with sickness. Makhan must have been really upset with her. Makhan's condition was not also very sound. Her husband somehow managed to have two square meals a day. Even that also stopped from the moment he had fallen ill. He had three young daughters in his house. All his pennies were exhausted. But the real problem arose after his funeral ceremony. People in his neighborhood somehow managed to complete his funeral ceremony.A good amount of rice was collected from every household. Even some amount of rice remained after the funeral ceremony. From that unfinished rice and grams that were collected at the funeral rites, he took away two kilos of rice and some grams to give them to Bili. Taking away the packet of items from Makhan, Bili thought if she should have taken this stuff from her elder sister or she should have offered them instead.

Makhan's son Nagen was talking endlessly with Mohan and Rajen in another room. Mohan and Rajen started pouring in dry grams from their pockets one by one, the grams which their maternal aunt had brought for them and listened to the tales told by Nagen. They had to suffer for food. Again they enjoyed feasts also. His elder sister stayed in the professor's house in the town. They gave her fifty rupees a month.

But that amount was too spent in purchasing medicines for her father. Sometimes feasts were held. Nagen said that there was no dearth of items after their father's death. People offered them many items to consume at home. Rice, grams, bananas, dusts of Pithas - innumerable items. Items piled one after another. One could hardly eat all those bananas - they were bored with bananas. Apples and grapes reached their home from the house of the professor where their sister stayed. I had never experienced grapes in my life - Oh, What fun! They were as big as the seeds of the 'Bakul' flower. They were very tasty. I had taken apples earlier. Once my sister took them from the professor's house. Many food items were collected. Rice was collected to a great extent. Also, there were grams. Today, whatever she took with her, she took them from that collection of items. Death of a person was always good - people would bring many food items. Every person brought at least something with them.

"Why do they give, after all?" Rajen at once interrupted in the middle of the conversation.

"They must give only. It is said that none should visit the house of the dead without carrying some food items. So, every person carries something with them." Nagen said and Rajen did not reply to that.

They could fill up their empty stomach with rice after a long while and so all of them slept nicely. Before the sleep, one thing kept moving in Rajen's mind that people took items in the house of the dead people.

The elder sister of Bili went away the next day saying that she would come again. While going away she suggested that she should be informed by someone as and when it was required. Bili put a bowlful of boiled rice in front of Narayan's mouth from the rice that her elder sister had offered her. She had not added salt to it. Narayan did not take it near his face. Bili rebuked her husband. Once Narayan took the bowl and started to drink the water and developed a hiccup. He continued his hiccup and vomited at last. It was said that such hiccups were common with the patients of urinary infections which developed swelling. Bili felt sorry for that. She only wanted to make him eat the rice somehow by scolding him. That proved really troublesome for the man.

Two days after that Narayan died at about 9 o' clock in the morning. Their houses were filled up with people from the neighborhood. Narayan was left on the yard on a banana leaf facing the east side. Even they had no cloth to cover the body of the dead. Bili tightly gripped the body of her dead husband and started weeping in an uncontrollable way. The condition of the people in the vicinity was the same - none had a piece of new cloth in their houses. Akan, Narayan's elder brother rushed fast to his home and brought a previously bought piece of dhoti (lower garment) from the provision store and put the cloth over Narayan's body by tearing it apart into two pieces. Mohan and his younger brother Pravin were lying glued to their maternal aunt's chest. Rajen was not there. Nobody asked his whereabouts. Everyone seemed to have forgotten him.

Many people assembled carrying sickles and axes in their hands. The yard was full of people. Narayan's immediate elder brother seemed terribly busy in arranging the items that might be asked as soon as the brahmin priest arrived. He also carried some money in his pocket. He knew it well that Bili had no money with her. Some men went to the bamboo grove at the backyard to cut the bamboos. The bamboos were also only a few there. The elder brother of Narayan called Jaduram to send some men to cut a few bamboos from the backyard of his house. The front yard of Narayan's house was crowded with many people like a current of water on the river. Two of the women tried to drag Bili away from the dead body of her husband. Rajen was standing under the 'nahar' tree in front of the gate of the cowshed. Rajen seemed to be unaware of the fact that his father had been lying dead in the yard and his mother had been crying heartily. He did not take rice yesterday in the afternoon, he felt really hungry from within. His belly was demanding some food.

Rajen was looking out towards the hands of the pole approaching their home. He did not look at anybody's face. He fixed his attention to the hands of everyone. Rajen ran on the road as soon as his father was taken out from the room and placed in the yard. His mind was free to know that his father had been dead but he was soon upset to see the hands of the people coming to their home. He was looking at the hands of the people.

Then Rajen dragged the hand of Biren who was coming quickly to their home and asked him innocently, "Brother Biren, shouldn't one come to the house of the dead carrying bananas, grains, etc in one's hands? When my elder uncle died, people carried some items on their hands. Don't you know that one should visit the house of the dead carrying something in one's hand?"

Is it Time?

"They have entered for self-defense, not to defend the country."

"Which way are you going? Is it time?"

"You can hear the guns shouting, not the birds."

The door was closed but not hooked. It made a strange sound when pushed. Many persons were sitting. The sister and both the sister-in-laws were also sitting. Everyone was shocked. One looked at his watch, it was one o'clock. Paran entered and passed a smile looking at everyone and stood at the head of the bed where his mother was lying. Uncle Nanda who was reading the kirtana sitting on the ground finished reading and looked at Paran. Everyone came to a halt for sometime.

His mother's eyes were half open. The mouth was half open too and made sound while breathing. Paran couldn't decide whether she was sleeping or was in coma. He asked the sister-in-law standing beside, "Is she sleeping?" His brother answered, "She has been in the same condition for two days." Paran kept quite. He touched his mother's eyes and sat beside her. The night was long and cold.

"Wherefrom have you come today?" His uncle asked.

"From Naharkatia,"Paran said.

"Who gave you the news,"Uncle Nanda asked.

"I got a letter a few days earlier from her."Paran said looking at his elder sister.

"I sent a letter with Jagannath," his sister said trying to paunch the mosquito sitting on her mother's forehead.

"I have some work here tomorrow. Otherwise it would not have been possible to come." Paran uttered as if he was doing the most unimportant and meaningless job of his life. Everyone kept quiet in the room. They did not know what to ask or say.

"Pour some water into her mouth,"Uncle Ridhai told Lavanya. Paran took the water bowel from Lavanya's hand and poured some water in his mother's mouth.

Paran gulped down the **pithaguri** and the banana his sister-in-law gave. Lavanya was astonished. Since their mother fell ill, her thoughts had been revolving around Paran. She was thinking that Paran might howl like a baby. It was because their mother loved him more than others. Two years ago he left home. Lavanya felt that made their mother more ill. At first their mother thought Paran went to study MA. She got the news from one of their cousins. She suffered from insomnia and headache and got bedridden. Lavanya thought Paran would start crying as soon as he saw his mother. But nothing like that happened. He was gulping down the **pithaguri.**

"Now I realize how hungry I was. I had three chapattis in a line hotel near Chepon at 9 o'clock,"Paran said chewing the food. For a long time no one talked. Suddenly Ajmal, who was sitting in a chair near the door asked, "Why did not you eat anything after that?"

"I had no money."

"What! You had no money?" His friend Nabin asked him alarmingly.

"I was given just 3 rupees as eating expenses for the day,"Paran said.

"Is three rupees enough for one day? Was there shortage of money?" Bharat Morang asked.

"There is no shortage of money at all. But the allowance for daily's food is rupees three," Paran answered him. They kept quiet for a long time. After finishing his food Paran washed his hand and wiped out with the **gamosa**.

"You are doing some very good work. There are no drunkards in our village anymore. No one even plays card. I have heard it has been happening throughout the country. Very good! But there is a great problem. The boys who broke the wine shops themselves smelt of wine. These things will harm you." Uncle Nanda daringly told the things and looked at Paran. Paran laughed and said," It has been happening at places. We are watching them. Either they will correct themselves or they will be eradicated. There are rules for it. Introducing members at random was our grave mistake. Therefore a lot of unnecessary people have entered. They have come for self-defense not to defend the country."

"You are doing a very good job. If wine and gambling can be uprooted only then the country will survive, otherwise it will go to hell," Uncle Ridhai said.

Uncle Ridhai told Uncle Nanda to read one more section from the kirtana. Everyone looked at the woman sleeping. Paran leaned against the wall sitting on the stool. He tried not to sleep. He had not slept for the last three nights. Morning was a few hours away.

Although he was a wholehearted participant of the movement, he passed his B.A. with distinction. Lavanya passed out two years earlier than him. Their father passed away almost seven years back. He was in Dibrugarh for three months, but was not cured. How could you expect someone who was suffering from cancer to be cured? It was very costly. We had to pay separately for each 'ray'. Even the professors had to be paid for the allotment of seat to the patient. The oldest of all the brothers was a primary school teacher and the second one had a small business. Everything was settled. But problems started after the death of the oldest brother. A grant of 30000 rupees would have been given had they produced the certificate of a martyr. Even Shiva Hazarika; who died in dysentery had been given the certificate of martyr. His nephew himself was the President of Students' Association and was very close to the President, Gana Parishad. Grant was given to him. But their brother Sibam Thakur died in police firing. A polling booth was established in his school. He opposed it and went to the booth and ran out holding the ballot box. The guards shot immediately. The first shot hit his hip and the second pierced his chest. He died on the spot. It is not that only their brother died in '83. Why should he go to others for a certificate then? Does the sun need a certificate? Paran was against it. No one cared for them. They promised a job for the families of the martyrs. Still, Lavanya did not get the job of the clerk. The post was given to one of the Town Committee's Chairman's relative. She did not even get the post of a teacher for not paying bribe.

There was celebration everywhere. The boys had formed the government. There would be happiness everywhere. There would be no foreigners, no bribery, no price hike and no corruption. The security forces too would have to respect the common people of the land. In this condition they had gone out. But where did they go? Neither Prabhat nor Lavanya could understand it.

People came looking for Paran after a year had gone away. The Town Committee's Chairman, the MLA, the councilor, the President of the ruling party everyone came. They didn't approve the path that Paran chose. They could have given Lavanya a job if they wanted to. But how would they afford to give Lavanya a job leaving their relatives out? Lavanya looked at Paran. She wished to tell Paran many things. Both the sister-in-laws were also looking at Paran. Prabhat was sitting still. Uncle Nanda was reciting lines from the kirtana. Nabin and Bharat were trying to discuss their plans with Paran. The situation was bad. If only he could have stayed for a day or two!

Would he be able to stay? The police must have been reaching by now. The most corrupt minister was warned thrice. But he didn't care. Later, his head was found in a bag and the body was never found. Security forces had gone mad after the incident. They arrested people indiscriminately.

Lavanya wrote in detail to Paran about the condition of their mother. She might be suffering from stomach cancer. She desperately wanted to meet Paran. He would not be able to see her if he didn't come soon. She thought Paran would come home after getting the news. After a few days Paran replied. He said that he did not have time because the 'Great Mother' was also suffering. They were trying to save her. If she could be saved, the mothers in our houses would itself come out of all the troubles. She would not have to suffer anymore. "We have come out too far. There is no way to go back," Paran wrote.

Lavanya became angry as well as felt sorry for Paran. He would also turn into a dead body someday like their brother. It would be better if their mother died before all this. Lavanya just wrote two sentences to Paran, "In which way are you moving? You are keeping your life, present, future, and everything at stake. Is it time?" But now when Paran himself was present in front of her she wondered if it was time for her words?

Everyone including Uncle Ridhai had jumped up. There was a strange sound coming out of their mother's mouth. She was finding it troublesome to breathe. Each and every time she inhaled her eyes blinked. Paran stood up and Nabin opened the door. Uncle Nanda tried to find her nerves. The elder sister-in-law ran to the kitchen to bring a glass of milk. Suddenly she screamed. From all the sides the long rays of torch light had flashed. Lavanya also entered and started to scream police, police. Paran searched for something in the bag hanging from his shoulder. He looked around the room. "It's time," Uncle Ridhai said. Uncle Nanda has said, "Nabin, Prabhat, help me."

She was laid down on a banana leaf. Lavanya and both the sister-in-laws were wailing. People had gathered in the yard and surrounding them were the police. They had searched the compound. A few of them had run towards the mango tree and fired a few rounds.

Lavanya raised her head and looked around. She didn't see Paran anywhere. Could he cross the forest? Had he not left instantly she would have told Paran to leave?

But Paran himself had left. Not much time was left for sunrise. Morning didn't come with chirping of birds; the morning dawned with gun fire.

Glossary

Pithaguri: Rice powder.

Gamosa: A piece of cloth that is used for menial chores.

My Son

My son.........

Have you seen my son anywhere? He went away at the midnight hours. Once he came home. While I was observing him top to toe he said," mother, if there is something, please give me to eat. I am very hungry." He said if there is something. Lest he would come. Lest he would call, "Mother." I always saved some food for him. If there was scarcity of food, I saved my own portion. I told my daughters that I was not hungry or I was ill. But he never came. In the next morning the sisters had to take that dry boiled rice. That day also I saved some food for him you know! And he came. All of us kept looking at him without the blinking of an eye. There was scarcity of kerosene; still I kept a lamp full of oil aside lest he would come at night. I had lit that lamp and looked at him. Why won't I? For how many days he had not come home. Not days, actually it had been years. He said mother if there is something...... I had given him some rice. The boy washed his hands and started eating without changing his clothes. All three of us were looking at him. When he was eating a shameless thought occurred to me. If I tell it now people will say that the old woman is exaggerating. I felt like my son had turned into a ten months old child and was suckling sitting on my lap. Suddenly he raised his head and tried to sense something. Then only we realized that a motor vehicle was proceeding through the village road. He jumped up and ran to the back door. In darkness he just said," it's the police be careful." We had started panicking and stood still as if hit by a thunderbolt. One of them immediately put the plate and stool in a corner. They had surrounded the whole house you know. The boy went away at midnight. Have you seen my son? Have you seen my son somewhere?

Don't ask me what happened that night. I had just passed third standard in a village school. I hardly knew anything. They searched the whole house and started interrogating us. "Where is your son?" We said," we have not seen him for many years." They said, "you are lying. He had come just now. We have confirmed news of his arrival. He is at home. Where is he?" We said, "He is not a coin whom we will put in our purses." They had turned the three small rooms of the bamboo house upside down searching for him. Some of them spoke Assamese and some Hindi. The girls earned by weaving. They had broken the whole set of the loom. The girls got furious. They tried to protect it. They now caught hold of the girls. I could sense the ensuing disaster. I put my lamp down and started pulling them away. How could I prevent those strong men? Someone kicked me on my belly and I fell down. I had become senseless. For some time I had heard the girls shouting. A few moments later they started groaning. I had tried to get up but felt giddy. I had felt uncontrollable pain.

The news was given in the newspapers. We could not read it. It's because we didn't have a newspaper. I had heard from others. The news was given in the newspaper. Have you read it? Is it given in detail? One of the girls could not open her eyes for twelve days. The other one bled for almost three months. Were these things given in the newspaper? I had to sell my goat to pay the doctors for treatment in government hospitals. Was this also given in the newspaper? After the incident, people feared coming to our home. That night Bhabesh, who was once my son's colleague, informed the police. Have you read these things in the newspaper?

At midnight hours my son came. Have you seen him somewhere? I have not seen him for a long time. I wish his father is alive!

His father had named him Krishna. It was Janmashtami when he came to this world. And what a co-incidence, his father was assigned the role of Nandaraj in the **Bhaona** in **Naamghar**. His father was about to leave when the pain started. Gongai's wife at once came and cut the umbilical cord. His father could not play the part and gave Tapohdhar the responsibility. Therefore, his father named him Krishna. I called him, "My little one." The first one was a boy, next were two girls and finally Krishna, my little one. You may say I am fabricating. Reading the horoscope the purohit said,"Bubai, your son will behave like Krishna one day. He will kill asura. Wish! His father were alive. It's better he is dead now. Otherwise he would have been very sad. His daughters would have been molested in front of him; his son would have fled at midnight and police would have harassed him like anything. But he had suffered a lot. Such a harmless man should not have suffered so much. Why won't he? We have no land of our own. He worked in the land of others with might and main. Doctors said it was gastric ulcer and told him to shift to Borbari. But we could not. He just vomited blood. Nothing went down his throat. At the final stage the man swelled. One day he whispered in my ears, "It's so painful. My death would have saved both of us." A few days later he died vomiting blood. He toiled very hard to get both the boys educated.

Have you seen my elder son? His name was Biren. Don't you know him? After passing matriculation he was unsteady. My father-in-law donated the land for a minor school where at present the high school stands. His father supplicated the headmaster insistently to give him a job. But all went in vain. The headmaster finally agreed to give Biren the job of a watchman when he promised not to take salary for five months. He served near about two years. Bought a **bigha** of land within those two years. He wanted to buy some iron sheets. His father stopped him saying you can by those at any time. Why don't you buy some land? He hanged himself when his father was alive. People said he did not commit suicide. He had been killed. The truth was never found out. He went with the headmaster to bring the salary of the school staff. On the way back they had been robbed. He whispered to his father that it was the headmaster's conspiracy. The police harassed him after that. One morning he was found hanging in the mango tree behind the school. The land was donated by my father-in-law. It was given in the newspaper. His father found the news. They are gone now.

Have you seen my son Krishna? I call him my little one out of love. Have you seen him somewhere? My little one!

He was good at studies you know. He passed matriculation in second division. Passed B.A. too. During the movement his friends left studies. But he continued and passed B.A. His friends beat him up accusing him to be an anti-movement worker. They accused him of being communists. We were boycotted by the society. They threw stones at our house. Those were all his friends. He was humiliated in college. He was even dragged to the jungle to be killed. Somehow the police got the information and rescued him from their clutches. Otherwise, my little one would not have lived. The police not only rescued but also protected him. The police who once protected him are now after him. Things are so confusing. I just understand nothing. One day his sister Lavanya asked him, "once your friends were after you and police protected you now it is reversed."

Why is it so? He answered nothing and just smiled. You know after so many days he came home that night. He even could not finish his food.

Have you seen him searching for a job? After passing B.A. he searched for a job for many years it is said. His companions had formed the government. His sister used to say why they would give job to a communist like you. He said," I am not begging for a job. I shall compete for it." He did not get one. Both his father and elder brother were dead and had two sisters to get married. Had they been married off then this would not have happened to them. Sometimes he told his sister that he was not getting a job just because he didn't have money to pay bribe, not because he was a communist. Friends are taking bribe from their friends for jobs. But before forming the government their agenda was that jobs should not be sold in the market.

After that he remained absent from home now and then. Sometimes he did not come home for six months or a year. If he happened to come home there was always someone with him. They just talked and read. He just did not bother about us. Sometimes in his absence police c ame to our house. They told us that he was a traitor.

He was killing people. Can such a harmless boy kill someone? Where had he got gun? Who had given him gun? Whom was he killing with the gun?

Why was he killing them? Maybe he was killing those corrupt people. No. I can't believe what the police are saying. Moreover who would believe them? Had my little one killed people unnecessarily, would he be saved by public? On the other hand, they were providing him shelter.

One day he told me, "Mother, you don't worry for me. Wherever I go, I find a mother like you. They also take care of me as you do. I have gone out to wipe off the tears from the eyes of all of them."

Have you seen him somewhere? I have not seen him for many days. Is there anyone who will understand my agony? From that midnight I have not seen him yet. I am searching for him. Once in Bhaona, I saw a mother hiding her child in her womb lest somebody would kill her baby if she gave birth to it. If I find him, maybe I too can hide him in my womb. This time I won't let him go.

I was searching for him. Disturbing you by repeatedly asking about him. Look! My son has returned this morning. I know although he talks about many mothers he cannot forget me.

I know my son will come back to me. That is my son. His father named him, Krishna. I call him my little one. Look! He is sleeping. He is brought in the police van. They have kept him in the yard. These girls - how could they be so cruel; how they dare disturb my sleeping son. Don't shout! He will wake up. At midnight he went. He has not come home after that. He must not have slept for nights. Oh dear! He is sleeping so peacefully.

Sleep my son, sleep. Was there so much blood in his body? All his clothes are drenched in blood.

I was asking you about my son without any reason. My son has come long ago. He is sleeping. Don't disturb him. He is sleeping peacefully.

He is covered with blood as if he has taken bath with blood. It's so red. That's why my son is surrounded by the policemen. I know my son will come back to me one day. My son.......

Glossary

Bhaona: A performance of a one-act play on the premises of the place of worship.

Naamghar: Traditional Assamese prayer houses.

Bigha: Way of measuring land.

No Dirt in the Heart

Sometimes certain thoughts prick our conscience continuously like a nail that is stuck in our shoe sole without our knowledge and keeps on giving us pain. In the silver jubilee year of Indian independence this thought was continuously pricking me.

I was a lecturer in a training institute then. It was at Joysagar. The place was good. I lived in a government quarter. Every Saturday a man cleaned the latrines of our quarters. He was a cleaner in the municipality. While leaving after finishing his work the man found me sitting in the verandah reading. Every day the man put his wet broom under the armpit and conveyed me regards. I was then a young man of 25. I noticed the eyes of the man glittering and there was a glimpse of deep intellectuality on his face. No one would have bothered if he had worked as a cleaner in a socialist country. But in a money dominated democracy like India his position surprised me. It's because if we clothed him well he would look like either a professor or a government officer. My curious nature made me talk with the 45 years old man. I lived in the quarter alone with a peon for company. The man was at first surprised as I tried to converse with him. Later, he talked with me well. Yet, he maintained some distance with me. He never sat on the chair. He even hesitated to sit on the stool. He washed the cup in which tea was offered to him. This particular behavior of him made me uncomfortable. But I kept quiet thinking lest it should make him uncomfortable if I told him to stop these.

After our marriage the man maintained a distance from us. But later when he found Pranati no different than me, he became comfortable with us. He cleaned the backyard after cleaning the latrine without our knowledge. He plucked olives from trees for pickle. Once there was a strike of cleaners. He cleaned our latrine at night during those days. Our friendship developed and few of my colleagues mocked me for this. But the only person who showed interest and felt special about it was Abha aunty. Her heart was like us then.

His name was Amru. Amru Singh a Punjabi Hindu by caste. Let me tell you about Amru Singh. Amru was 20-years-old then. He was the only child of his parents. His father died when he was fourteen months old. He lived with his uncles. They had enough land. So he did not have to worry. 20-year-old Amru could never think that earnest appeal of Gandhi's non-violent method would ever win India freedom. Therefore, he joined the **Azad Hind Fauj** with a few of his friends. His mother tried to stop him. But he vowed not to listen to anybody.

During the Second World War, Amru was in Burma. It had been four years since he left home. For inevitable reasons **Ajad Hind Fauj** was broken. Soldiers like Amru were at sea after the incident. Amru started working in a cloth store, fell in love with the owner's daughter and got married. They beget two sons within two years of marriage. In the meantime, India got freedom. Amru was very eager to come back to India. He had plenty of fertile land in his village. He appealed to the Indian government for passport and visa. But there was no response. Later he wrote letters to the Prime Minister, Nehru every month but without any success. He personally wrote to the Home Minister, Sardar Vallabbhai Patel. It seemed the heart of the iron man had also turned into iron. Amru was getting crazy to come to India. Having left with no other choice, Amru took permission from his wife and in-laws and decided to smuggle into India. He promised them as soon as he reached India he would arrange passport and visa and take the family to India.

Amru's mother fell unconscious as soon as she saw him. Within these years she had grown old. They thought Amru to be dead in the war. So his cousins registered his portion of property in their names. Amru's mother too agreed to the proposal and signed the documents. Amru had to face many hardships to smuggle into India. He even had to pay bribe to security forces at the border. After so many hardships what he found was that he didn't have a piece of land in independent India. Amru's mother cried embarrassing him. After a few days Amru declared, "I will work as a cleaner for a living. I am not ashamed to work freely in this free country. I don't need this property these are all dirt."

His struggle started again. He had to struggle for passport and visa to bring his family from Burma. For this he paid bribe in almost every office of independent India. He ended up all his money in this, yet he was not able to get the visa and passport. After many hardships he met Nehru. Nehru heard him for two minutes, wrote something in a paper and handed it to him. With much hope he gave the paper to the officer. The officer wrote something on the paper and stuffed it in the basket near him. He went to the officer for almost a year but without any success. In between his mother died. It had been eight years since he left his family in Burma. He was very eager to meet his wife and sons. He borrowed some money from his friends. Amru decided to stay in another country leaving his own independent country giving bribe to the security personnel in the border. Amru reached Burma after nine days. He almost ran towards the house that his father-in-law gave him.

Two boys were playing a ring in the yard. They must have been ten or eleven-years-old. They asked me whom I wanted. I was sad. I remembered them, they did not. They took a few steps back and called their mother. She was astounded to see me. I too froze. She said crying that she waited many years but finally she had to submit to her parent's torture and had to marry another man. She had a son from that man too. I did not wait there anymore. I wanted to touch the boys. But they did not put a step forward even after their mother's order. I came back. Instead of going to Punjab, I came to Assam. Since then for the last twenty years, I am cleaning dirt here. Saying this the man stood up and conveyed me regards and went away. While going he hummed, "Sare jahan se achchha, Hindustan humara........" That day after Amru went, I sat in the same place for almost a hour. I felt belittled in front of that man.

In the beginning I said that something pricked me from within. But it is not this.

After that I felt more close to Amru. He sometimes borrowed one or two Hindi books from me and at times read it to me. In the meantime my little daughter who had just begun to articulate started calling Amru as uncle. I had seen many a day Amru's eyes filled with water when my little daughter called him uncle with her babbling voice. But one thing that I noticed was that although Amru played with my daughter for almost an hour yet he never took her on his lap or touched her. Pranati told him many times yet Amru never touched her.

It was the festival of Holi that day. Pranati went to market with Ava aunty in the afternoon. I was sitting in the verandah reading. My daughter was watching some pictures. Once she shouted happily as uncle. I looked up and found Amru standing near the gate. The little girl ran to the gate. Amru was smiling. I called him in many times but he did not enter. He never came in if he was drunk. So I stopped calling. The little girl called him in. Amru came to the yard opening the wooden gate and gave her a twenty rupees note and said, “This is for you. Have some sweets.” The girl took the note. I stood up astonished and shouted, “My dear, you are not supposed to take the money. Please return the money to uncle.” She offered the note to Amru. Amru went two steps backwards looked at me with his red eyes and said, “Sir, I clean dirt. There may be dirt in my hand. But I have no dirt in my heart.” He went away like a bullet. The little girl also froze on the spot with the note in her hand.

This seventeen years old incident still pricks my conscience. In the golden jubilee year of India’s independence, Amru is disturbing me very much.

No Need Then

The driver had slowed down the car, looked back and stopped a little further. Opening the back door, MLA Chandra Mudoi had got down. His two companions and the driver had also got down of the car. It's five in the morning. Four-five people had gathered. They were brushing teeth. The MLA asked a man passing by, "male or female?"

"Looks like a female," the man replied and passed with speedy steps.

"Let's go, we will get late otherwise. We have to reach there at 6 o'clock."Mudoi ordered the driver. His companions had agreed with him. The driver started the car.

In the back seat of the car they were discussing the scene that they had witnessed just now. They were discussing whether it's a good omen to witness such an incident early in the morning. Mudoi remembered he had seen the cleaner Kumud before coming out of his house. Mudoi knew that it's a very good omen to see people like cleaners, cobblers, etc while setting out for a journey. His companion Jadav Tamuli had corrected him saying that nowadays using words like cleaner, cobbler was prohibited. They should be called 'Harijan.' Mudoi grinned, "You are right. They should be called 'Harijan.' It is just a slip of tongue that I called them by that name. It will bring disaster if I use these words in meetings. Is it a good sign to witness such a scene?"

A person was run over by some vehicle. The road had been smeared with blood. Blood clots had spread here and there on the road. Strangely nothing of these were found on the spot. Must be a very poor man! Still he was alive and walking till the moment he was hit by a car. There must have been blood is his body at that time. What had happened to the blood? MLA's other companion Nabin Gohain who was also known as a socialist uttered, "There is news of some man who drank blood. Have they done it?" They all nodded in agreement. But the man sucked the blood of children not adults. But the most important thing is that is it a good omen to witness such an incident. The only person present who had the knowledge of all these was Jadav Tamuli. They had turned to Tamuli. Tamuli had said that he had long forgotten all these. Anxiety spread over MLA Mudoi's face.

He had the right to be anxious. He was teaching Physics in a college before being elected as an MLA. He would have retired after five months; instead he was elected for five years as an MLA. He had captured the whole solar system in his hand in the form of rings. He had fourteen rings in his ten fingers which signified the nine planets. Before being elected as MLA he had seven rings of various stones for seven planets. They had helped him to be elected as MLA. Other seven rings he had gathered during these five years. Just two months left to complete his term of five years yet he had not been able to get the post of a Minister. Sometimes he felt like throwing away all the rings. But astrologers said it took time to show effect in some cases. All his dreams would come true even if he got a good department in these two months. He had even convinced the Chief Minister to take the gem stone of his choice. He hoped that it would soften the Chief Minister's heart towards him. The Chief Minister also had the whole solar system in his hand. It would make the universe if we put the stones of his waist, arms, neck and hands together. He had seventeen rings in his fingers save the amulets. All these had worked for the CM. But nothing was working for unlucky Chandra Mudoi. Still, he was hopeful. If he got an important department just for two months, it would prove very helpful for the next elections for him **start.**

Mudoi had been very anxious for the last three weeks. The newspaper said he had been flattering the Chief Minister. He did not see any fault in him. He was the first to protect the Chief Minister with mother's affinity from all kinds of criticism. His criticism started with the most respectful words found in the dictionary leading to most invalid words available. But when he could not manage a berth in the cabinet after the seventh shuffle of the cabinet, he had lost all his patience. Burdened with sadness and anger he had exploded in front of his colleagues saying, "I have so long protected Chief Ministers corruption and in return has lost everything. Now, I will expose him." His colleagues had presented it in front of the Chief Minister making a mountain out of a mole hill. The Chief Minister was dissatisfied. They started avoiding Chandra Mudoi. But the heartrending news was that he had decided not to give Chandra Mudoi ticket for the next elections. From that day Mudoi had lost his sleep. There could not be any greater insult for a Minister or MLA than denying him ticket for the elections. It's better to slap him in public than doing this earlier. Mudoi understood that nothing would work until he showed his power. This was the preparation for it. People from a revenue circle had organized **Guru Tithi**. The circle fell under his constituency. When they had come to invite him as a Chief Guest, he had instantly accepted their invitation and donated two thousand five hundred rupees. He had again promised to give two thousand five hundred rupees more on the day of the programme. While leaving his house the young principal of the newly established college had suggested, "Sir, elections is near at hand. It will be better if you can attend the early morning procession. There will be a gathering of eight to ten thousand people irrespective of caste, creed and religion. Last year there were eight thousand people and we travelled four kilometers. This year the number will go up. It will be very beneficial for you if you join the procession." Mudoi had started his preparation as the well-wisher principal suggested. The High School teacher, Jadav Tamuli had given him an essay on Sankardev prepared from various note books. He had halted for the night in the dak bungalow twenty miles away so that he could reach there on time next morning. One could enjoy life in a dak bungalow. Gohain and Tamuli had also stayed with him. With much enthusiasm and hope they had started their journey early in the morning. But after witnessing the dead body he had been disheartened. Was it a good omen or bad to witness a dead body while setting out for somewhere?

The scene had made Chandra Mudoi anxious. The reporters from newspapers and TV channels, photographers, etc would be present in the function. The news would be featured everywhere in the newspapers, TVs and radios. Let the Chief Minister know his power. If only he could get an answer for this. Jadav Tamuli had forgotten all these and there was no point of asking Prabin Gohain.

Chandra Mudoi himself wouldn't have believed lest the Chief Minister should believe it or not. There was a five to six kilometers long line of people. Almost fifteen thousand people had joined the procession. Out of those fifteen thousand people, twelve thousand would be regular voters. Lots of people had gathered in the meeting too. The organizers had said that they had a budget of two lakh rupees for this event. The Ministers who were invited had not understood the importance of the meeting. Their absence had highlighted Mudoi's importance.

Chandra Mudoi had given a good speech. People clapped in between his speech. Mudoi had again promised to give seven thousand five hundred rupees more in the name of the organization.

The priest Ashutosh had got much more than he had expected. His face was glowing in happiness. He was discussing with others about the meeting. But Chandra Mudoi had been thinking just one thing. He was worried whether the Chief Minister and his followers would come across the news and photographs. Mudoi had not only told about Sankardev in his speech. He had criticized the economic condition of the people. He had criticized by saying that a class of people was growing richer and another class was growing poorer day-by-day. It's not that he had told all this for the sake of speech, he really felt for the poorer class of people.

"That means it's better to witness a dead body while setting out for somewhere," Jadav said.

"Oh yes, I have forgot the whole matter throughout the day. It's better to witness a dead body while going somewhere. It's proved today. We have reached the same place isn't it? It was near the police station." Chandra Mudoi said looking through the window.

Strange! A few people were still gathering there and the dead body was still in the same place. Chandra Mudoi got down from the car. His companions had also got down. The dead body was covered with flies. A policeman was protecting the dead body from the dogs. One policeman came to the MLA and asked, "Sir, is there any problem?"

"This dead body is lying here since morning."

"No sir, we have informed the cleaners. They must be reaching. He has no relative."

"Whose dead body in this?"

"A beggar, sir."

"Oh, no need then. Let's go."

The MLA sat in the car. The driver's hands were shivering while driving. He looked at the dead body. Ten years ago his beggar father was also run down by a car like this. Who knows this dead body was also one of his relatives.

Glossary

Tithi: Birth or death anniversary of saints or famous personalities.

Now

Bedlam broke. The first person who saw it was the peon of the Circuit House. It was early in the morning. Later the news spread like a storm and brought the people of the city towards the Circuit House. A huge crowd gathered. Security personals were seen everywhere. This happened only if some Prime Minister or Chief Minister visited. The District Commissioner had himself called and sent an Additional District Commissioner to the Medical College situated three kilometers away. But the Additional District Commissioner had to return from its gates because the Principal of the College with a team of specialists had set out for the Circuit House. The Principal had arranged everything in lightning speed. Someone was in the toilet, someone was brushing teeth, and someone was in the bed with his wife enjoying the laziness of the winter morning. But all of them had reported instantly the moment they got the news. The Principal gathered his team of specialists and teachers and proceeded to the Circuit House.

In the Circuit House, the District Commissioner himself had to set to work to control the crowd. In the meantime the team of specialists had reached the Circuit House. All of them had entered in the room almost running with the District Commissioner.

The bed was very big and soft. A big man was lying on the bed. The team of specialists set to work immediately. The District Commissioner was observing them.

A team of foreign trained specialists had taken more than half an hour to declare the same incident which a compounder of a Primary Health Unit could declare in ten seconds. They had examined each and every part of the body. Everyone knew the result yet no one was willing to voice it. The Principal looked at their eyes and said looking at the DC, "Sir, already dead." At the same time he had said that the person died almost two hours ago. The DC without wasting a moment dialed a few STD numbers. He first of all informed the Chief Minister, then the Chief Secretary and finally the family members. He ordered the SDO Sadar to suspend the staff of the Circuit House. The staff of the Circuit House consisted of the receptionist, the peon, the watchman, the cook and the gardener.

The dead person was a powerful minister. In his opinion and according to others he was the next Chief Minister. The powerful Chief Minister was afraid of him. He said he could be the Chief Minister within six hours. But he did not want to be. His work life would be an ideal for the sluggish Assamese youth. Like Karmabir Nabin Chandra Bordoli his biography should also be included in the curriculum. His biography would give inspiration to the frustrated Assamese youth. They would be able to learn from it. Everyone would support the proposal if they got a glance of his eventful life.

He came here almost two and a half years ago. He was fifteen then. He worked as a boy in a goods truck. He had left home quarreling with his family members and went back twenty years later in his new ambassador car. Although he was only fifteen, he was powerful and well built. Marwari shopkeepers liked to keep him as a record keeper or gatekeeper in his shop because of his physique. The climate of Assam was allergic to work and that is why he had stopped doing that kind of work. He started working as a boy in a hotel. Though the hotel wasn't big yet it had the capacity to compete with some of the best and posh hotels of the city. There progressive items of the modern day that is liquor, women and gambling of all kinds were available in the hotel. Disagreement and quarrel followed these three things. In this condition well-built people like him were in great demand. So the owner of the hotel had appointed him as 'Boy'. The owner had paid him hundred rupees more than others. His perseverance had made him a manager of a country made liquor shop. While working as a boy he had learnt to write his name with lot of persistence although it looked like a big fountain pen. He had developed intimate terms with the famous people of the land. He had tried to speak the Assamese language but could not succeed. Yet, he called himself an Assamese by heart and soul. He could not study much and he had no regret for this. He started commenting that, "Goddess Laxmi and Goddess Saraswati don't like each other. Therefore, when one stays in your life the other one leaves you." His life justified the statement because the boy who left home at the age of fifteen in a goods truck had returned home at the age of thirty five with a beautiful wife and a brand new ambassador car. Other than that the boy who worked as a ' Boy ' in a hotel had become the owner of eleven liquor shops. He owned three big hotels in three big cities and three palace-like buildings. He had become powerful too. In matters like whom to give party ticket or whom to take in the cabinet, his opinion always mattered the most. He was popular also. Leaders and ministers of all the political parties, leaders of students' organizations and even some of the surrendered revolutionaries visited his house. Didn't these parameters made him enviably popular? Finally, he had decided to take part in the elections. Before his second wife came to know about his wish the political parties were scrambling over one another to give him ticket from their party. He had responded to the ruling party, won the elections and had become the minister with his chosen departments. As a minister he was in the second place of the cabinet. No criticism had been able to put any effect on him. Should not the biography of such a man of extraordinary quality be included in the curriculum? Should not the Assamese youths be inspired reading it?

The same person was now lying dead in the bed of the Circuit House. Would not there be a panic situation! Orders had come from Dispur to finish the post mortem promptly so that his family members and those who were coming from Dispur didn't have to face the hassle. His dead body was taken to the medical college. The DC and the principal had also gone with the dead body.

He did not know what tiredness was! He died last night. But the whole day he had continuously given speech in a meeting organized on the occasion of **Liquor Prevention Week**.

He had given speech in Assamese and since his grasp over the language was not so good; he had to face lots of hardships. He had been an avant-garde in the matter. He was a very humorous man. The DC, ADC, Sadar SDO, various leaders and noted personalities were with him till almost twelve last night. What a vibrant man! They had gone out of the room after he had fallen asleep. The DC had closed the door from outside while leaving. Such a man of inexhaustible vitality was found dead in the bed at 6 a.m. Wasn't it strange? Had somebody killed him or had somebody poisoned him. None of these was possible. The post-mortem report would tell everything. There was not a minor sign of injury. How could he be killed?

Message arrived that the Cabinet and the family members would be reaching within an hour. The DC was thinking where the dead body should be kept for the final tribute. He could not decide whether he should keep the body in front of the court building or in the Circuit House. He was anxious imagining the reaction of the CM. The DC was somewhat sad for his sudden demise. He was powerful and had supported the DC's nomination for IAS. The principal came to the DC with an envelope in his hand. He handed over the envelope to the DC and said, "Sir, the report, if you want any changes."

"Why didn't you tell me?" the DC said to the Principal.

"Sir, brain hemorrhage."

"Brain hemorrhage? Why? "

"Sir, he was suffering from high blood pressure. There was pacemaker in his heart. He drank too much of wine that day. Due to high blood pressure his nerves got broken and as a result he suffered from brain hemorrhage." Both of them kept quiet for sometime.

He could be called a martyr. It was because in the **Liquor Prevention Week** he gave a speech in fifteen liquor prevention meetings in one day. But at night he died because of over drinking. Was there any other person on earth who had set examples by dying in the **Liquor Prevention Week** - no not at all? Therefore, he was a martyr.

On the Bank of the River and the Bridge

"For the last few days, we had been figuring each other out, Isn't it?"

"Yes, we have been meeting here at the same time since long and looking at each other."

"If our eyes meet then we look towards the river in front of us or look over the bridge."

"Yes, we look but don't talk."

"Just a minute. Since I have started talking first then I would like to ask you a question. Can I ask?"

"Please do ask. Not one, you can in fact ask many questions."

"Yes, even if we cannot answer still we may learn."

"We can silently contemplate. Isn't it so?"

"Yes, yes we can think over. Please do ask now."

"There is nothing particular but only one doubt. Can you tell me why we keep on coming to the bank of the river and we return after looking at the river. Can you really tell me the reason?"

"Then I can add another point to it. Can I? Please do so."

We sat on the bank of the river. He was asking why we always stood on the bank of the river. But I wanted to add another point to it.

"Just wait. I shall tell. Can I articulate the point that you want to add? Can I tell?"

"Please do tell."

Actually he wanted to say that we did not merely stand on the bank of the river, rather without our knowing we went to the bridge above and came back on the middle. We almost tip-toed while going but walked faster while returning.

"Yes, you are absolutely right. How old are you?"

"I do not know why the question of age surfaced here?"

"You cannot certainly understand because you are a female. Do not think that I am undermining the potential of women and I certainly do not mean to. Women are in fact more intelligent than men."

"But –"

"But you probably want to say that either an old woman or a young female equally feels embarrassed regarding the question of age. Isn't it so? What is your opinion?"

"Then I have to describe my age now. I am seventy two years old."

"You are an old woman. Yes, you are indeed an old woman."

"All of us are aged. None of us is below seventy years. I am seventy five."

"I am seventy seven."

"And I am seventy four.. I raised the question of age to verify whether people belonging to the similar age feel similarly or think similarly."

"Then there are two questions. Why do we come to the bank of the river and return half way from the bridge."

"I have not understood anything. I am not intelligent enough to reply. My head is dull and it has lost its sheen. Do you know that I was a watchman of a school? When the government provincialized it, I had only nine years before retirement. I got salaries of these nine years but did not get pension."

"Can I then say first? Do not think that I am very intelligent. I retired as a teacher from an L.P School."

"Now you can reply to the question. Why do we come to the bank of the river and return halfway from the bridge."

"Can I narrate my individual viewpoint?"

"Please do."

"Have you noticed one point? Just look."

"What?"

"Even though we are aged we are males. We are men. But even though we are aged, there is a woman among us. But have you noticed how that young woman is providing milk to the child by openly displaying her breast."

"Yes, but you should also see how that boy is playing with her left breast. That means he also wants breast milk. But the mother is unwilling to feed him."

"They are poor. They live near the railway station. They sell out plastics."

"Yes I have understood that they are poor. There are two questions involved here. First, why has the woman come to the graveyard along with these two children? And the second point is related to her conduct. Why is she openly displaying her breast in the midst of males? This has no connection with poverty. Isn't it so?"

"Then you have overlooked one point."

"What point? I did not notice probably. Will you tell?"

"Why? Have you noticed the white folded cloth in the hand of the woman?"

"Yes, I have noticed. You will mark the same cloth as a protection against cold tomorrow. Because of the torn saree, isn't her back exposed?"

"I have understood. But why is she not wearing the cloth in her hand? What is her intention?"

"Why is she roaming like this?"

"At least she can warm up the piece of cloth."

"Why?"

"Now I have understood that we have only grown old but have not learnt the process of thinking."

"Yes, we are absolutely right. Otherwise we would not have come to the bank of the river daily without fail. Do we climb over the bridge?"

"Shouldn't we finish the discussion regarding the woman carrying the folded cloth?"

"Listen to me. Look that is a crematorium. It has got fencing and something is also planted there."

"Kindly remember, yesterday we saw the crematorium and we also marked the piece of white cloth tied to the four plants."

"Yes, I have understood. This woman has taken the cloth from the crematorium out of shyness."

"Yes, but not merely today and not only this woman. Have you marked any white piece of cloth in any of the crematorium here?"

"No, I have not seen."

"Have you noticed other attires thrown away along with the dead body?"

"No, I have not noticed."

"Look at these boys and girls, they are searching something in the midst of ashes at the crematorium situated on the north. Just look at them."

"I have marked. But why?"

"Because some wealthy people offer gold and silver along with the dead bodies. They do not burn in the fire. That is why these boys and girls are scrutinizing the ashes in order to get hold of gold and silver."

"After knowing all these I want to say something as a woman. I want to talk about the young woman feeding her child with breast milk."

"If you do not mind, then please tell. Even though you are old, still you can make us understand better because you are a woman."

"People who struggle to get their meal do not have shame. Please keep on noticing another point besides this. This child is chewing the breast in order to mitigate his hunger but does the hard breast have milk?"

"Yes, you have pointed out something important. One who has taken away the cloth of the crematorium and whose elder child is chewing the hard breast out of hunger."

"Does she have her husband?"

"It does not matter whether she has husband or not. Rather her problems will multiply if she has a husband. Her misery will increase. It will definitely increase."

"You are absolutely right. The husband will be lustful at night and as a result of that another child will be born to chew the rough breast of the woman."

"Your point is meaningful."

"But aren't we diverting from the main issue? Yes, we have indeed diverted our attention."

"We are analyzing the reason of our going to the bank of the river and coming back halfway from the bridge. Isn't it?"

"Yes."

"Then we should discuss that. Who will tell first?"

"I shall begin as I am the eldest here – seventy seven. Even though all of us are above seventy, yet I am the senior most. Isn't it so?"

"Yes please begin."

"What is left to be said?"

"Why? You told that you would begin. Didn't you say?"

"Yes, I told. But anyone can read any page of an open book. Such a book attracts the attention of everyone."

"I could not fathom what you said. Didn't I say that I was a watchman of an M.E. School who did not get pension."

"Yes you told so. I probably did not say, I was a clerk."

"But I was a mother. Yes, a mother."

"There is none above a mother."

"But to a mother there is nobody who is above her children. Do you know?"

"Won't you give me the opportunity to ask? Didn't I want to begin as the senior most person?"

"There is no doubt that you wanted to begin but you also raised the issue of being an open book."

"I am dragged. I wake up at night and keep on waiting to hear the whispering of birds."

"Why?"

"Because I can go out of home imagining that it is about to be dawn."

"If you forgive me then I want to ask a question. Where is your home?"

"In the heart of the town. Near the petrol pump. It's about four kilometers from here."

"What was your profession?"

"I was a lecturer. Lecturer of philosophy - have you understood?"

"You are a professor. I have not been able to convey my regards to you even after such a long time."

"Have you noticed that I keep on looking at the anthill of the public crematorium staying near the bank of the river."

"Yes, yes, I have marked. Sometimes I wanted to get introduced to you and also wanted to ask you. But please tell why you keep on looking at the anthill."

"Those are tombs. Crematorium."

"Whose?"

"It's of my wife and my beloved."

"What are you saying – professor of philosophy? You had a wife as well as a beloved."

"It's natural. One may have. Even though I am a woman, I can cite many examples."

"Do not undermine the point. Do you know how much I loved my wife?"

"But she ditched you? Isn't it?"

"Yes, I was jilted. She squandered away all my hard earned money. I also did not get pension. Both of her kidneys were damaged."

"That's why you did not say that she betrayed you?"

"Yes, I am right. She died leaving me alone. Can I tell one thing?"

"In fact you are talking."

"She was not sad that both of her kidneys were damaged. But she was a broken woman because of the neglect of her son and daughter-in-law."

"What do your son and daughter-in-law do?"

"Both of them are officers in the sales tax department."

"I am sad to hear that. Probably we should have felt sympathetic towards you. But if you want to clean the table with a wet cloth, will it dry up? I just want to place this question."

"Yes, understood. But what about your beloved."

"Feel lonely at home. I always come to the bank of this river and see her. It grew into a jungle. It turned to green. In front of my eyes, the tomb became an anthill."

"In the midst of that there is the context of the beloved."

"While coming here regularly, I got the company of an old woman. She was also tormented by her son and daughter-in-law. She told so. I developed compassion for the old woman whom I met during my morning walk. Can't exactly tell when we fell in love."

"It's really surprising. Does not love know barrier of age?"

"I also thought earlier that love is related to a particular age."

"Afterwards?"

"We always met at the bank of this river."

"We spoke out our hearts. Both of us felt sad on the day we could not meet. Felt dizzy. But suddenly three days passed since we met. On the fourth day, I decided to slowly walk to her home and thinking so, I came out of my home when there was still darkness. The clock struck five, six, seven – but she did not come. After some time I decided to go to her home. At last she came. She crossed me on the shoulder of her two sons. What was surprising that she was cremated near the tomb of my wife."

"Did she die?"

"Yes, she had a heart stroke. She died after three days. I looked as her body was cremated which took almost three hours. I was looking at that from the bridge. Have you understood now why I keep on coming to the bank of this river?"

"Your tale should sadden us. Even though it is late, yet we express our sadness."

"Since the last seven years, I have been coming to the bank of this river in order to see my wife and beloved whose tombs are now covered by greenery."

"Have you noticed that he is crying?"

"Women feel sadness with more intensity and weep soon. We have a woman among us. We should not forget that."

"Suddenly an old woman was crying. Isn't it our duty to ask her why is she weeping. We are also old."

"Wait, I shall ask. Why are you weeping? Please tell why you are weeping suddenly."

"Probably the sad tale of his dead wife and beloved did not make you weak enough to weep. An old person having inner strength."

"No."

"Then? Please tell us why are you weeping?"

"Do you hear the sound of mother's broken heart? Have you heard the sound of pain a mother feels? Do you know how the heart of a mother burns?"

"What are you saying?"

"I studied up to class five in an M.E school. I do not know the art of speaking nicely. Apart from that I am a woman."

"Do not weep then, but you have said nicer things. You are talking of the sound of a mother's broken heart, of the pain of a mother's burning heart."

"Have you marked the past in the middle of the bridge?"

"Yes, I have."

"I was tied below the water. It became rotten. It was torn and remained hanging."

"What? Who are you talking about?"

"My son."

"Your son!"

"What did he do? Will you tell us?"

"He was a member of ULFA."

"ULFA? Was he educated?"

"He passed M.A. The father sold a plot of land and provided for his education."

"Is the father alive?"

"No, he died."

"Who killed your son and tied him to the pillar of the bridge of the river?"

"His companion did so."

"Who were his companions?"

"They belonged to the ULFA group. I again ask whether you have heard the sound of a mother's broken heart and also the sound of the mother's burning heart."

"The answer to what you are asking is inside our heart."

"Did he take part in the movement?"

"Yes, he did."

"Did he get any job?"

"No, do not misunderstand my son. If he would have got a job, then he would not have turned out to be an ULFA."

"Are you sure that the rotten corpse of a boy in the water happened to be your son?"

"Does a mother recognize the blood of her son? The murderer of my son himself confessed his crime."

"How far is your home from here?"

"That I don't know. It is situated in the northern part of the village. It takes almost one hour to reach here. I have a burning and broken heart. That is why I do not know what I say. People make fun of me as they call me a mad woman."

"I always come near the river. I look at the pillar. I get its smell. I can smell his body."

"Do we need to tell that we are sad to hear your tale?"

"You are an aged person. The mother did not weep when she told you about the rotten corpse of her son. But listening to that tale you wept folding the head beneath the knee. It is a truth to say that there is hardly any distinction between a child and an old person?"

"Please do not misunderstand. I did not weep listening to that tale."

"Then?"

"I heard the sound of the broken and burning heart."

"Hers?"

"No, mine. I heard the sound of her broken heart like broken pieces of object made of clay. I smelled her burning heart like the smell of a raw fish."

"Abruptly?"

"No, I got hints. I severely beat my daughter. I used a cane to beat her."

"Where did you get the cane to beat your daughter?"

"I told you before that I was a watchman without pension. I used to plow my own land in order to reap harvest. Then should I look elsewhere for a cane?"

"Yes, it is natural for you to have. But why did you beat her. How old is she?"

"She was twenty eight then."

"Was she educated?"

"Yes, she passed B.Sc. Do not think that I am exaggerating because she happens to be my daughter."

"She secured first division in matriculation examination and got better marks in Science and Mathematics."

"What sort of father you are? Graduate – a mature girl – you should not beat her like that. Doesn't he deserve to be criticized for his action? "

"I am a mother. I did not weep initially when I saw his rotten body and when I saw different parts of his body hanging. But in spite of being an old father, you are weeping by stooping."

"When did you beat your twenty eight years old young daughter?"

"It's almost four years."

"Even after four years, why should you weep like a small child?"

"I always keep on weeping."

"But we have been seeing you for a long time but we never saw you weeping."

"I weep inside, It resides in my heart. I suffered from gastric ulcer and passed black stool. I was given blood. Do you know?"

"Was she your elder daughter?"

"My only child. There was no second child even though she tried hard."

"It's really a sad tale. Only daughter.... But afterwards?"

"Should I tell?"

"Please tell. But if you don't mind – I am asking because you said – you told that she was pregnant!"

"Yes, I told."

"Not for once. But for twice."

"Twice she became pregnant, first when she was in class nine."

"It's strange to hear. A girl of class nine becomes pregnant."

"Will you explain a bit?"

"Yes, I will, But please give me some time. I want to compose my mind by crying. Please allow me to weep."

"We are also old. We are also getting aged day-by-day. In front of us an old person will weep, it might look odd."

"Don't we need to look at him?"

"Please do not tell him anything. There is no use. Haven't you noticed how he has been affected by sorrow? He is crying from the core of his heart."

"It's like an old tale resurfacing. Please tell us openly how she was pregnant in class nine. Because your daughter is also our daughter. That is why it is imperative for the father to know."

"She took part in the movement. Used to obstruct oil at night in groups. The leader who made her pregnant was also responsible for the abortion of the fifteen-year-old girl as told by her mother."

"Then you beat her."

"No, I did not. Do you know the leader became a minister later on."

"Will you tell anything more? I too have something to say."

"Yes, I will. I have to tell you about him. She also went. She saw the father who survived without pension suffering. That is why she went along with the minister. She roamed around the capital. Did not get a job."

"If you do not mind, Can I ask a question?"

"Please ask."

"You told that the girl who used to roam around the minister managed a job. But your daughter failed to get a job."

"Am I wrong to ask you this question?"

"No, you are right. It's better to ask him these questions. We would understand better."

"Please do not mind. Because you do not know the company around you asking question. "

"It's so? How?"

"It's not nearly enough for a young girl to go with a minister and sleep will him at right."

"Then?"

"You also have to bribe. But the rate was lesser in case of my daughter - fifty thousand."

"But why did you beat your girl?"

"Please allow me to shed tears. My heart is heavy with grief."

"Is it proper to allow him to weep like that?"

"It's not immoral. Tear drops will wipe out his grief."

"You could say such a good thing only because you are a professor."

"I did not feel ashamed to say that she went to the capital along with the minister. The minister forced my own daughter to sleep with him but gave the job to someone else ultimately."

"Apart from giving herself, she probably gave money also."

"Yes you are right in your assessment."

"After that?"

"When she started crying and used abusive languages against the minister and mistakenly she disclosed that the minister was responsible for her destiny- she was also pregnant for four months."

"The old man wept and could not tell anything."

"It will be a bit better to let him weep."

"How long shall I weep? How long? I did not weep that day. Rather, I did not beat her with a cane. I never beat anyone like that."

"It was not fair to beat a young girl of twenty eight years."

"What did her mother – your wife – do then?"

"She tried to resist me. The mother knew the secret beforehand but did not tell me, that is why I beat both of them."

"It was not proper to beat an old woman. Did he do the right thing?"

"But why do you come to the bank of river almost daily for the last few years?"

"Why did you return halfway from the bridge? Will you tell?"

"I shall get peace if I tell. The daughter did not come out of the room for two days and did not eat anything. But on the third day the mother noticed that she was not in the room. There was great hue and cry. People came and went. At last police provided the information."

"What did the police inform about?"

"Look I am pointing at the spot – she was hanging there. She was hanging on the rod of that bridge."

"Oh, Oh, that means she committed suicide."

"She jumped off the bridge. Her slippers were there. Whenever the day broke, I came near this bridge to see her. Though sometimes I could not come, I remained there in the bed of my room as I felt dizzy."

"We also felt like crying along with you after hearing this tale. But did not you feel tired by crying for such a long period."

"Don't you know that there are two sorts of weeping?"

"Yes, I do know. I practice both types of weeping. Don't disturb me. Let me weep a bit."

"Then we were getting tired by talking and crying. Our feet were also trembling. The old man was sad regarding this."

"Should we end here for today? Shouldn't we go back now."

"Why shouldn't I disclose the reason for coming to the bank of this river daily in the morning? I climbed the top of the bridge. Then I returned halfway. Won't you listen?"

"Yes we have to. Why won't you tell? Please tell."

"Can't I start?"

"Please do."

"If I would have got strength and power then I would have demolished this bridge."

"You are not talking like a old man, rather you are talking like a terrorist. What is this?"

The boy felt intoxicated and went away. He did not get the job of the clerk at the block office from where I retired. His interview was satisfactory. But rather the job was given to the son of the immoral councilor who got compartmental in matriculation exam.

Nowadays the scenario of the job is everywhere like this.

I scolded him because he failed to manage a job and made fun of him as he was eating free of cost at my home.

"Don't you think that it was not proper on your part?"

"I did so in order to make him active. One day he simply vanished. The mother and the sister were displeased with me."

"Where did he go? Did he commit suicide?"

"No, he did not. He joined the armed forces in order to wipe out corruption from the country. One day he felt disillusioned. He returned home after five years. He told that the people who wanted to wipe out corruption from the country were themselves corrupt. We felt good. He opened a shop near the college. He was attached to his work. He opened his small shop near the college from where he graduated. He did not feel ashamed."

"Your son was intelligent enough to do so."

"I have been coming to the bank of the river and near the bridge since last six years."

"Why, will you tell us the reason?"

"The mother was possessed."

"Possessed?"

"The mother was possessed from five in the morning till nine. She became a completely different woman and became terribly angry."

"She abused me. She did not know what she did at that time."

"Then?"

"Then she became dumb from nine in the morning to five in the next morning."

"Why did the woman become almost mad at that point of tome?"

"Not like mad but she became a mad woman. Because at that time they discovered the body of my son."

"Where?"

"Below the bridge of this river."

"What? Did he commit suicide?"

"No, he did not. They murdered him and his body was thrown in this bridge."

"Who murdered him? Who killed your son?"

"Those with whom he wanted to wipe out corruption from the country."

"Why did they kill him?"

"Because they doubted that he gave information to the police and military. The dog of the police discovered his body around five in the morning below this bridge of the river. Now you tell me, shouldn't I demolish this bridge? Please tell when he gave information to the police and the military."

"Look we have been crying here for a long time. Have you noticed how the people passing through the bridge are staring at us?"

"I have thought something, Can I tell?"

"Please tell, you are the oldest among us and apart from that you are a professor of Philosophy."

"Should I disclose the real feeling of our heart? Why should we come here?"

"Please tell, we are getting bored by weeping."

"Actually we always come to the bank of the river to see its flow; it may wipe out our grief, like the non- stagnant water of the river. We, the motionless want motion in life."

"But the bridge?"

"I shall tell you. We want motion, we want a bank. We want that bank but we feel afraid, we return halfway from the bridge quicker. We want movement – we want bank – that bank."

"But ....."

"Look but ......"

The Mother is Everywhere

Entering the new house after three months the woman started crying. The two-roomed house was made of bamboo and roofed with tin. For the last two months the woman called Khudmai was crying. Entering the new house after three months the woman started wailing in such a way as if her child had died just now The man was puzzled. Other three children were standing near the grandmother feeling puzzled. The grandmother was muttering, "what's the use of wailing now? It is destiny. Take care of those who live."

Chaos started. Fire, smoke, sounds of gunfire, hue and cry of people could be heard everywhere. Everyone was running here and there. The fire from the burning huts had illuminated. People had cried relentlessly. In this condition, someone was laughing like a Ravana in a **Bhaona**. People were even running through the jungles and fields. People had tumbled down while running. The old and sick people who could not run had started shouting. Kids were shouting.

Khudmai and Bhekola were getting prepared to sleep. They were daily wage earners, they went to bed as early as possible. Khudmai had just come in after washing the utensils in the pond. At that time hue and cry started - sounds of gunfire could be heard - there was fire everywhere. Before they understood something people started running. Slowly the noise went up. Everyone in Khudmai's house also started shouting. Bhekola immediately took the dao and a son with him and went out. The old woman tumbled down. Khudmai also took two of her children and joined the crowd. The woman had tumbled down because of their tangled clothes. In the chaos no one could be heard of. No one knew the whereabouts of their family members. No one knew for how long they were running like that. Electric bulbs had been lighted around the school field. People had started crying in a huddle.

Stopping under the tree suddenly, Khudmai put the child on her lap down and started wailing overwhelmed with grief. Bhekola, his mother and other three children had stopped near her. No body had come near them. Because everyone was crying for their own reason. Khudmai was wailing beating her breasts. Bhekola and his mother stood puzzled. All of a sudden their tiredness had taken the shape of terror and wonder. Slowly, Bhekola's old mother sat down and started wailing. When both the woman had started shouting, "Son Manuh," Bhekola thought what he should do. Would he cry too? But he had not and sat down.

The woman had cried till dawn. Bhekola wanted to go but other people had advised him not to go. Everything had turned into a heap. Everyone including the police had informed them that not a single stray dog was alive in those villages, only the remains of the burnt houses were left. There was hatred among the people against the Nagas. After the incident it had further intensified. News arrived that the son had escaped hurling his mother in the pond. Many grown-up boys and girls in the fear of Nagas escaped wherever they could. Although no news of them had come, but the elders were thinking that they would come back. But Khudmai and Bhekola had never thought that their eight months old son would be found ever. Khudmai started howling the moment she remembered him. Later, Bhekola got irritated and scolded his wife, "Your wailings will not bring your dead son back!" She kept quiet. The thoughts of her dead son was pricking her mind. How could she do this? How was it possible for her to leave her son behind? It would have been better if she would have died in the hands of the Nagas. At least she wouldn't have to suffer such agony. She couldn't discern in a hurry. Out of fear she took Gereli and Son Manuh and started running. After stopping in the school field she realized that instead of Son Manuh she had brought the pillow with her. She had left her son on the bed.

Just before raining the sky turned cloudy. Everyone got to know. Such a havoc had rocked their life but nothing had changed. "What's our mistake? Did we do any harm to them? Both of us drink from the same river, buy goods from the same market. At times they come down from the hills and rob our house but we have never gone up the hills. How could they do this to us?" The people in the camps discussed among themselves. In the camps many people had fallen ill, many had died. Many woman had delivered there.

After three months, people had left the camps. The government had built new small houses for them? A few had criticized that the Nagas had given the government a chance before the elections. A healthy minister had visited the refugees. "The Missing, Bodo, Ahoms, Muslim - these people were more simple than Assamese people," said the minister. A few officers present there had thought - this minister even does not know who is Assamese in our land.

After three months entering in the new house Khudmai started wailing, beating her breasts. Bhekola felt sad, instead of getting angry.

Next morning, Khudmai started searching for something in the backyard. Both her husband and her mother-in-law was watching her. The children were also helping her. Where would she find any trace of her dead son among the ashes of her old home? He must have burnt like cotton. At that moment Deukan informed Bhekola. He had returned home from the camp ten days ago. He said that he had heard the news in the market. Khudmai came near him. Bhekola stood puzzled. He could not decide what to do. He started thinking with whom he should discuss the matter. Unintentionally, a smile spread on Khudmai's lips. But at that very next moment it turned into a cry. Bhekola thought it would have been better had the news not reached them. Now, he had to face many troubles.

Undone! Finding himself undone Bhekola had told everything he had heard. He had to go with the woman in the morning. Khudmai also wanted to go with him. The Naga hills would be far, but she would go in search of her son.

Khudmai, Girikanta and Bhekola set for the journey. They had got the news that it was in the foothill of the Naga hills. Both Bhekola and Girikanta were afraid. But Khudmai showed courage. Some advised them to take the police with them. But Bhekola did not. His logic was that since they had not harmed anyone why would others harm them.

They had reached the house. Khudmai heard some children crying in the yard. She saw them. But it is not her Son Manuh.

The man described everything in Nagamese. "They are fighting. Killing people. Burning houses. I just wanted to have a look. Heard cry in the house. The little boy was crying very much. I brought him with me. The next day, I saw the houses burning."

This time tears rolled down from Bhekola's eyes. The Naga man called his wife and said something to her. The man again said that the child had not eaten anything for many days and had been crying all the time.

Khudmai had jumped up when she had seen the Naga woman carrying Son Manuh from inside the house. Son Manuh was crying. The Naga woman put her nipples in his mouth. He stopped crying and started suckling in utmost satisfaction. Khudmai should have cried. But the scene had left her puzzled. Her own child was feeding from another woman's breasts.

The man gave Bhekola a new pair of cloth. He bought it for Son Manuh. The Naga lady gave Son Manuh in Khudmai's hands. But Son Manuh had not shown any interest in crying. Bhekola, Girikanta and the Naga man's eyes had also turned moist.

Khudmai had pressed Son Manuh hard against her breast. He had cried louder. The Naga woman took Son Manuh in her lap and put his mouth in her breasts. Son Manuh stopped crying and started suckling as if he had returned to his own mother's lap. Two drops of tears fell on Son Manuh from the eyes of the Naga lady. She said, "Bring him to meet me sometimes." She could not say anything more. This time both the mothers had started crying together.

Ours

Biman did not need to worry. After completing his B.A., he had got the very first job he applied for. It was the post of an inspector in a cooperative department. A small post of an Executive. But it was enough for him. He went to work from his own home, took his salary at the end of the month and submitted his T.A. bill. He was very satisfied.

Biman regularly sent letters to his beloved. He met her in a marriage. Her name was Ashima. A pretty girl! Of all the girls present in the marriage party her attire was simplest. There was no ornament on her body. They had fallen in love at first sight. Biman had to go to work. So he returned from the marriage ceremony next afternoon. She had told him to send letters in her college address. Ashima went to the university for further studies. Her address changed. But the series of letters and the topics in them remained the same. Biman wrote to her regularly and got reply with much regularity.

In the evening, after coming home Biman changed his clothes, took tea and went out riding his bicycle. He spent almost two hours with his friends. At about 8.30 to 9 p.m. he reached home. After getting married many of his friends had stopped coming to their gathering place. But Biman was an exception in this case.

Biman was a good man in conventional terms. He never thought of taking bribes. Instead, he tried to criticize those who took bribe. His comments went in this manner that in present social condition it's very difficult to survive without taking bribes. So it's a mistake not to take bribe. But he himself never took bribe. Ashima also never encouraged him in this matter.

Biman's younger brother was Bakul. He was an angry young man. He had completed his B.Sc. degree six years ago. Yet, he had not been able to manage a job. Nowadays, one had to bribe fifteen hundred to two thousand rupees for a government job. The present minister was a former MLA of the opposition party. He had given some jobs in concessional rate to the boys who had helped him in elections. Some of them had bribed twelve hundred rupees for a teacher's post. Bakul had abstained himself from all these. Nowadays, he read books and magazines of communism. Sometimes he told Biman to bring books and magazine from Jorhat. Biman informed him if he did not get it. Sometimes, Ashima also wrote the names of some magazines, books, etc and told him to read. He wrote back, "I enquired Bakul about the books and magazines you told me to read. He told that he had two. I will read as soon as I get time. " Bakul became astonished when Biman asked him about books and magazines.

Biman regularly read **'Illustrated Weekly', 'Statesman', 'Desh'**, etc. He read Assamese magazines like '**Amar Pratinidhi', 'Prakash**', etc. too. **'Prakash'** was a very standard magazine. Articles and other writings were also good. Bakul had nothing to say in this regard. But he felt irritated when Biman praised the story written on Krishna's death. Not always, but at times he argued, "On which ground you call it good? What message is there?" Biman became speechless. Still he tried to reply, "You don't find any message in our magazines, in the same way, we also don't find any message in your magazines." Bakul gave a satirical reply.

Biman didn't regret. He was happy with everything. Their union was fighting for pay rise. "Let them fight. Wherefrom the government will give salary?" Bakul's party was giving pressure on the government for the prevention of unemployment. They were accusing the government. The numbers of unemployed youth was fifteen lakh. Was it possible for the government to create fifteen lakh jobs? It was easier said than done. There was not a single unemployed in China. In a country of eighty crores there was not a single unemployed person. At present the population had reached to almost ninety crores. Bakul corrected instantly. "They have solved the problem of unemployment. Everything depends on production and distribution. Is there not a single beggar? What happened to the beggars? They have killed all the beggars." Bakul replied, "Have you seen them killing? Our holy places are beggar places. But in their country they have employed the beggars in proper work. They have not left it to God like our country. After all where there is no God, there is no problem, "their oldest brother remarked. "In the godless country people don't suffer from hunger, they have their luck in their own hands." Biman remained speechless. Bakul felt pity for him. After sometime Biman said, "Bakul, are these things written in your books? Give me those books. I want to read them. Please, mark those lines for me. Otherwise how shall I find it?" It's hard to believe what Bakul had said. Not a single unemployed person? In 1962, Biman was in his pre-university classes. China had attacked India.

There was news in the newspaper that China had attacked India to decrease their growing population. Indian soldiers had killed thousands of Chinese people. Bakul laughed loudly. "A war to decrease population! Who attacked first, India or China? Do you have any idea how many Chinese people those Indian soldiers have killed? Please, read these things. Think about it. You are a college graduate; educated person. Think your own."

Biman wrote to Ashima in the morning. "Why there is no reply for such a long time?" Nowadays, Bakul went out early in the morning. He was working hard for some cultivator's organization. Biman was friendly towards his mother. She loved him. But she was anxious about Bakul. "What Bakul is doing Biman? He has become a communist. Why should he ruin his life? Such a young man! He should have joined some government job. Is there no job of a graduate too?" Biman liked to talk to his mother. "You know mom, someday your name might be in books. Socialist leader Bakul Duvara's mother was Sibani Duvara." "Don't make fun of me."

In the evening, the atmosphere of the house was heated with discussion. Bakul, his three friends their oldest brother; who was a primary school teacher were busy discussing. They were discussing an article published in a weekly. **'Namashya'** was the name of the article. The writer was a former leader of leftist think tank, literature, professor, former Chief Secretary of Assam Sahitya Sabha - **Navarun Bora**. He was a very famous writer. He even noticed a small spelling mistake in letters. Very conscious man! At present he wrote thoughtful articles. Public opinion was on his side. He had written articles eyeing on some important aspects of the society. They were having an argument on that. They were opposing the writer and their brother in supporting him. Bakul and his friends were accusing Navarun Bora to be a very reactive person. For him leftist and progressive people were supporters of the foreigners. Like Bakul, his friends were also unemployed. That's why they were very sharp with the tongue. In their opinion, **Sahitya Sabha** was worthless. It had done no good to the land. Had they been able to maintain the social unity? Social unity had been destroyed because of their extreme point of view. Miris had taken up Roman scriptures. Bodo-Kacharis had taken up Roman scriptures. The society had broken. They were accusing Assam Sahitya Sabha of all these. Their oldest brother was protesting awfully. Biman was afraid of supporting anyone. Whom would he support? He could not win an argument even with Bakul. Now there was three more like him. He would be badly defeated. The problem of immigrants had taken possession over each and every aspect of the land.

Assamese people had turned homeless in their own homeland. That's true. Bakul was also supporting it. All these were true. But had the leftist party or leftist people paved the way? Who had opened the door? Where the government was? Wealth, People, Power everything lay in the hands of the government. Why didn't they use it? Why didn't they restrict? Why were they not doing anything? Then why didn't intellectual persons like Navarun Bora accuse the government. Why didn't they give pressure on the government? Instead of doing all these they were commenting against the leftist. Scold them with vulgar language. They were avoiding the critical situation. It's just a politics of buying fame and name.

"Your left parties should have used this public consciousness of the movement in their favour as a technique. Why have not they accepted the positive side of the movement?" His elder brother had said these things. Bakul remained speechless.

"Your magazine has reached. But Jiban borrowed it from me. He will return tomorrow. I read it in office. What they have written is correct. Economy builds society. Society doesn't build economy. Economy comes first."

Bakul was looking at his brother. He was wondering what his brother had read, what he had understood. Why had not he understood till today that the root of everything was economy? Administration decides the rout of economy. Biman must have understood something. How that has happened now!

Biman had written to Ashima that he had understood many things. He wanted to read books. Yet, he didn't want to accept everything.

Bakul and friends were of extreme nature in everything. The articles, writings of their magazines were very sharp. Who will buy your magazines? Bakul kept quiet.

Seventy eight per cent of the people of this country are poor. How much true is that? How people are living then? Is it possible?

Biman's workload had increased. According to the governments direction he had to establish co-operative societies in villages. Officers had no time. They were busy in establishing cooperative societies and giving ready made lectures. To be free from poverty, cooperative was the only medium. The only alternative against adulteration and price hike was the cooperative movement. Every government cooperative officer had to establish at least two cooperative societies. Each society must have minimum thousand members. Otherwise the officer had to show cause for his incapability. The officers were trying to establish societies in their allotted regions. Biman had also established two societies and selling shares. He was astounded to see the poverty among people. There were rich people also in the villages. But poverty was twenty times more. What an experience!

"Who is there?"

"It's us. We are government officers. A cooperative society is established here ... The ready made lecture went on. The audience was quiet. Please buy a share. It will cost just eleven rupees. Everyone from the village has to buy. Buy it now."

The audience was quiet for sometimes. With much difficulty he had opened his eyes and looked at the government officers.

"You are talking about eleven rupees, aren't you? I have been suffering from illness for the last one and a half years. I have not been able to pay offerings to God because of the lack of a rupee. Son, if you kill all the seven members of our family still we won't be able to produce eleven rupees. For many years I have not been able to see eleven rupees together."

"Is it true? Oh my God - what a condition! The Ayurvedic physician in the same neighborhood has bought shares of a thousand rupees. A total of hundred shares! Yet, this person doesn't possess just eleven rupees."

It is seventy eight per cent or ninety per cent? The number seventy eight can be called wrong after travelling the villages. Actually it can be proved. Are they all blind? Don't they see? Someone should have shown it to them. Either with the help of maths or through drawing. How to do it? Who can do it?

Have you understood Bakul? - Has Jiban returned the magazine? Have you understood Bakul? I think we need more of these magazines. How many magazines of this kind are published? Who has borrowed our magazines? We have to assemble all these. Have to write to Ashima to bring some of our magazine when she comes.

Path

Krishna Barua had frozen in hischair. His behavior expressed as if he had seen nothing, heard nothing. Some policemen were babbling standing near him. Nothing had appealed his brain. He started doubting himself - whether he was the same sixty eight-years-old Krishna Barua or not. After the police left, the house was silent. He had heard his wife and daughter Rekha talking. He had not paid attention to them also. It was not the first time that police had landed in his house. In other cases there would have been a great commotion in the village to know about the matter. But today nobody had come to Barua's house after the police left. Mr. Barua was still sitting. He was sitting motionlessly as if he would be shot if he moved.

Krishna Barua felt irritated. He had stood up from the chair and went to the nearby room. The room had been turned upside down moments ago by the police. His wife or daughter Rekha had not yet started to reorganize the room. Standing on the door he had moved his eyes around the room. The books were scattered around the room. There was not a single book on the table. They had turned the bed upside down and had read the documents put under the mattress. There was a big envelope full of letters. Mr. Barua slowly picked up the envelope. It was yet not opened. He remembered that he himself had put the envelope a few days ago under the mattress of Anul's bed. He wanted to read the letter. He had looked at the envelope. The words, "From Pon" was written over it. Who is Pon? He felt curious. Should he open the envelope. He felt hesitated. Throughout his life he had never opened other people's letters. Why should he open now? But who was Pon. Is the person male or female? He started looking at the envelope so intensely that the girl called Pon would emerge from it and would start talking to him, "Father, it's me Pon, your Anul's beloved. We are together for many years. Our thinking is similar. We have promised companionship to each other. Like Anul, I am also a graduate. I too don't have a job. We send letters to each other. Would you believe father we have not met each other for the last four years. Still we meet each other through letters." God bless you my child - he had muttered.

Krishna Barua had put the letters in its original place. The books were lying flat on the floor. He picked up a book and cleared the mark of the shoe from its cover. He read the names; Emil Burns, Marxism. He pulled up another book and muttered its name, "What is to be done?" - Lenin. "My son, you are reading these books and I even don't know. They won't understand the value of these books. I thought you have turned into a naxalite. But you are reading these books. Why do they trouble you so much? You are neither a brigand nor a killer. Then why are they after you? Why do they vandalize your books? They won't understand your value. I have not met you for many a days. Sometimes at night I have conjecture of your coming home. Believe me I too thought you to be bad as the police thinks. This time whenever you come home don't go without meeting me. I have some important discussions with you. You have read Lenin's book but I too will tell you what we should do. Son, don't go without meeting me when you come home next. I have kept the letter from Pon under your pillow. I could have answered it had I known the address." As soon as the old man stood up his head started spinning. He sat on the bed to avoid himself from falling down. He remained seated almost for five minutes. His whole body started shaking as if he was inside of a moving vehicle. Anger was running through his whole body like blood.

The old man walked out hurriedly. He stood bewildered near his bed. He brought out something covered in paper from under the mattress and came to the drawing room. For a moment he stopped and looked attentively at the photograph of Gandhi hanging from the wall. Suddenly he discovered that the photograph was taken when Gandhi was crying. It's because his eyes were half closed and his lower lip was a bit hanging. Yes, Gandhi was crying. Till now Mr. Barua had been thinking that Gandhi's eyes were closed out of satisfaction. But in reality it's not so, he was crying. Mr. Barua felt irritated. He could not see Gandhi crying. He dragged the wooden stool near the photo and climbed on it. He removed the cover from the copper inscription and placed it above the photo of Gandhi.

This copper plate was given to Krishna Barua by the government. He got down from the stool and looked at it. He felt as if the words inscribed on the copper plate had started spitting on him. Mr. Barua had tried to save himself by covering his face with his hands. He had felt irritated. He jumped up like a volleyball player and pulled down the copper plate. He held the picture of Gandhi with both hands and started shivering. Suddenly, the beatings of drums, bells and sound of conch shells reached his ears from the neighbor's house. The sounds started piercing his ear. The photograph of Gandhi was turning heavier for him. He couldn't hold it any more. Like a child in panic he shouted, ' Rekha', 'Pon'. Rekha ran to the room perplexed. Seeing the shivering father she asked, "What's the matter father?"

"Please help me dear, it's very heavy, "the father said.

The photograph fell on the ground and broke into pieces. The old man knelt down near the broken photograph as if he was out to pray. His eyes were filled with tears. Rekha was watching her father motionlessly.

With moist eyes, Krishna Barua looked at Rekha and asked, "Dear, is the sound of drum and conch coming from Pratap **Gossain**'s house? It's Mahaashtami today, isn't it?"

Rekha kept quiet. The old man said again, "will I be able to lift the sacrificial sword?" The old man felt as if people were playing the sacrificial rhythm surrounding him. The old man stood up and went to the yard with his shivering legs and started walking towards Pratap **Gossain**'s house.

In Pratap **Gossain**'s house the sacrificial rhythm was being played. It was being played continuously. Rekha was watching her father moving with unsteady steps. She felt that everything was played with the rhythm of her father's steps. What would he do now? What would he do?

Protagonist in the Background

Holding the newspaper, sectional officer Jayantamadhab Goswami stood bewildered. He looked at the newspaper from every possible angle. But the more he looked at it the more his heart throbbed in fear. There was no point of being afraid of. The photo published in the newspaper was theirs. It contained a caption that "tireless work of the officers saved the river embankment eventually saving thousands of people from the clutches of flood." It would increase their name and fame. His name with the names of the Executive Engineer and the S.D.O. had been published with the photo. Seeing the photograph he should have been very happy like the other two. But the telegram that contained the news of his son's illness dampened his enthusiasm and made him sad. He folded the newspaper and put it away.

The more he looked at the photograph, the events which occurred three days ago started flashing in front of his eyes. The thoughts of the events had made him drowsy. The event had crept into his mind in this form.

"Sir!"

"Yes, Jayantamadhab responded without looking at the person."

"Sir, today I want to leave a bit early."

"Early! But why do you want to leave early? You might have to stay back tonight. You have seen the condition of water, haven't you?"

"Yes Sir, but - Haradhan paused."

"But what? Exclaimed Jayantamadhab."

" Sir, Ratan, Aanamu, Haridhan all will stay back for the night."

"So, why don't you? What's so urgent?"

"Sir, my son is suffering from fever since last Wednesday."

"Your son is suffering from fever? Why haven't you told me? Isn't he your only son?"

"Yes sir, he is."

"You can leave; but come back tomorrow morning if your son gets well. You know the conditions."

"Sir, I shall be right back the moment his fever comes down."

Jayantamadhab's mind raced back to the story of Haradhan's life. One day Haradhan himself had told his story to Goswami. He had been in Assam for almost twenty five years. He was from Bihar. Earlier, he worked as a daily wager in railway lines. While working there he fell in love with a signal man's daughter, Roopmati. Roopmati was very beautiful . From the station master everyone tried to woo her. Haradhan excitedly told this. Once the station master tried to molest her in absence of his wife. Many such incidents occurred in her premarital life which she uttered to his husband without any hesitation.

"Sir, you can believe an animal but never on earth believe a woman."

"What do you mean?"

"Sir, I had a dog. After eight days Roopmati had left me, I too quit the railway job. As I boarded on the train 'Ratu' tried to jump in. I could not leave him behind. He died a few years back."

"Why did Roopmati leave you? Jayantamadhab had asked with some hesitation."

"You can never believe a woman Sir, sighed Haradhan. I have never seen my parents. I even don't know whether they existed or not. Roopmati filled that void up. I thought, I could die in peace in her lap. At such time, I had come to know that she was in love with a fireman. When I confronted the matter with the fireman called Mahendra, he had produced letters sent by my wife to him as a proof. I felt like killing both of them. But since I loved her very much I couldn't kill her and neither the fireman as she loved him. After two weeks of the incident she had left with him. But she had my child in her womb. If only I could have met her."

"You have left the job after that, haven't you?"

"Yes sir, I have left after the incident."

Haradhan came to Guwahati and managed a job of a labourer with the E & D department. Again love knocked at his heart. This time he fell in love with Radha and got married. Unfortunately, during the birth of their first child she had to undergo an operation. She had lost the capability of begetting any more. This only son of his had been suffering from fever for the last four days and because of this Haradhan took a leave that afternoon from Jayantamadhab Goswami three days ago.

In his fifteen years of service Jayantamadhab had for the first time met such an honest and sincere labour. He did not have any objection. The sole motif of his life was to work. Seeing him work Jayantamadhab felt inferior. Above all, although he was a labourer, he didn't have any inferiority complex. Goswami often wondered what made him so honest and sincere.

Goswami intensely looked at the photograph in the newspaper. All of a sudden he had felt an unknown fear. A chaos had unleashed inside his brain.

Haradhan said, "Sir, I want to leave early today; my son is suffering from high fever." Goswami permitted him to go. On that evening the sky turned as black as charcoal. The Executive Engineer of the E & D department and the SDO came to inspect the embankment. The condition of the embankment was critical. A small crater would lead to devastation. Therefore, they had come again in the evening with torches in their hands. They had started walking to the East of the embankment. After sometime they had stopped finding a fire. They had proceeded silently. Lighting a fire with some cloth, a ditch was being dug. In that part a sack full of sand was dumped. They had noticed that water was oozing out of the embankment.

"Haradhan", Jayantamadhab called."

"Sir?"

"What are you doing?"

"The embankment is dripping water; so I am trying to repair."

"But, are you not on leave?"

"Yes sir, I just wanted to have a look. But when I reached I have found water dripping."

"Has the fever of your son subsided?" Jayantamadhab asked anxiously."

"No, sir, it has not yet. But it might today."

In reality had Haradhan been late, the river would have created havoc. It started to rain after sometime. The embankment was saved. After two days this photograph was published in the newspaper with the Engineer, SDO and Jayantamadhab himself. The caption below the photograph said, "... indefatigable hard work and adroitness of the officers ...." Goswami couldn't bear to look at the photograph anymore. He felt powerless. Trying to burn the newspaper Jayantamadhab stopped abruptly. With feeble steps Haradhan was proceeding towards his room. Haradhan stopped near the door. His eyes had assumed the colour of red chilli. His face was covered with almost grey beards. He looked at Jayantamadhab and called – Sir!

“Is it you Haradhan? Have a seat. Goswami uttered.”

“Sir, I have come to meet you.”

“What can I do for you?”

“Sir, I won’t come to my work tomorrow also.”

“It’s ok. You can take leave as long as you want. Moreover, the danger has subsided now.”

“Sir, could you lend me some money now? You will latter decrease the amount from my salary.”

“How much do you need?”

“A thirty rupees will do sir. I did not want to; but his mother remains adamant. So, I have to perform the rites.”

“The rites! The words suddenly blasted out of Jayantamadhab’s mouth.”

“Yes sir. That night the boy passed away at about 2 p.m. I was on the embankment till twelve Sir.”

Jayantamadhab Goswami’s head started spinning. He felt as if he was moving down to darkness. Darkness drew in front of his eyes.

Religion

It was drizzling. In the east it was thundering so much as if the sky might break into pieces and fall down on earth. The house was closed. It was a post office. There were already some people in the verandah and as it was raining people kept coming in leaving no room in the small verandah. The verandah couldn't house more than twenty people. The woman held the infant tight and covered the two-year-old with the torn sack. The boy groaned. He didn't have the strength to cry loudly. Almost a score of people gathered in the verandah. Yet, nobody was talking. There were six or seven women too among them. No one noticed from where they all gathered there. Suddenly one among them started crying. Everyone tried to look at her in darkness. No one could see anything. Another was trying to vomit sitting in one end of the verandah. He had tried to spit out the bitter taste of his mouth. Those who were sitting beside him were watching him vomit. Everyone was sitting quietly with the head tilting down. No one was talking or wished to talk or couldn't talk or they might not have anything to talk about at all.

The one who vomited sat leaning on the wall. He could not keep his eyes open. He remembered the dead bodies. The young girl who was found dead with the sack wrapped around her belonged to their village. They came to town three weeks back as their village was submerged in water. These days they had seen many dead bodies at the edge of the road, on the verandah of the shops. If the situation remained the same, I would die too within a few days. Thinking the young boy too vomited. Is it me alone! All of them who have gathered in the verandah will die. The two children of the woman should have died earlier. It's strange that they are still alive. He tried to see the woman and the son sleeping beside her. Her two-year-old son would die at any moment. A rattling sound was coming out of his throat. His mother didn't know that. The dim rays of the street light fell on the verandah. The woman had put one of her hands on the boy. Almost everyone looked at the rattling boy, yet no one came to him. If they moved, they felt as if hunger would kill them. The sound of the boy's throat stopped after sometime. The mother shook the boy once and started howling. Although the woman had cried loudly, yet the words had not come out so loud. She pulled the dead boy into her breast and howled. Anyone who looked at her, started pitying her. Someone among them had said, "What's the use of crying? Turn him down from that side of the verandah." Another had said, "No use of crying now. Tomorrow you will die too." The woman kept on crying. The one who vomited felt curious; he came near the woman. The dead boy wrapped in the sack was still lying beside her. The mother was still crying holding his dead body. He had pointed to the other child in her lap. "This one died even earlier," the one who vomited had said. The woman shook the child, "Yes this one is dead too." Now she started crying holding both the children. "Oh! The child in her lap has died even earlier and she doesn't know," someone uttered. The woman was crying leaning over her children. After sometime she started vomiting. Her mouth was filled with the same bitter taste.

The boy who vomited went back to his earlier place and sat leaning on the wall. He heard a noise in the west corner of the verandah and tried to look. He pinched everyone sitting near him and pointed towards the direction. "What is it Joyram?" One whom he pinched uttered. They all looked towards the direction Joyram was pointing. Joyram had said to the one sitting next to him, "Gubin, what's now? It's a good idea. Otherwise day after tomorrow we will die too." All of them had immediately agreed to him as if he had told what they had been thinking. Joyram had pulled out the dao from the bag. Gubin had a knife and he took that. Binanda didn't have anything - he was not sure whether Joyram would be able to handle the dao or not. Quietly he took the dao from Joyram. Their eyes were fixed in the corner of the verandah. Like a cat that is out to hunt some bird, Joyram, Gubin and Binanda proceeded towards the corner with stealthy steps. "You have to finish it in one go," Joyram said to Binanda. The woman was crying leaning over her dead children. Few more joined them from back - as if everything was planned earlier. Joyram, Binanda, Gubin and the other who had joined them were all proceeding towards the corner stealthily. "Have to finish it in one go" - was the only thought running in their heads. In the west corner of the verandah a two-year-old calf was sleeping. "Have to finish it in one go." They had already surrounded the calf.

Glossary

Dao: A large knife.

The Last Rites

Nowadays, Bikash did not visit his home in the village much. He did not like visiting the village. Some would term him as a coward. For this reason he felt unhappy whenever he visited the village. In spite of this, he visited occasionally. After not visiting for a long time, one evening at about 7 p.m. he reached home. His sister, sister-in-law and nephews huddled around him. His sister-in-law reproached, "Do you often forget that you have a home too ? You possibly forget us the moment you cross the gates of the house. I often wonder what will happen to you if we get you married." Bikash just passed a smile. He did not have any reason to explain to them neither he had a reply. If he wanted he could come home every Saturday crossing the fifty miles distance. Only his sister Amiya understood him. She said, "Do you know why he doesn't come home?" His sister-in-law replied,' "Maybe because he does not have a wife here." Amiya said, "No it's not that, it's because whenever he comes to the village he gets sad news everywhere. That's why he stays away." The sister-in-law said, "Oh! Do you run away in the fear of a earthquake?" All this while Bikash just smiled. He distributed among the nephews the apples that he brought. This was enough to satisfy them. The only thing that related them with Bikash's visit was that he brought something for them and secondly they could demand him some money on the pretext of not having something or the other.

He had just sipped tea from the glass, when his sister-in-law uttered, "Are you here because of Pona Dada's news." "Why? What has happened to him ?" "Oh! Don't you know? Pona Dada died."

"Pona Dada died? When?"

"It's all shocking! He was working in the field whole day long. In the evening, he complained of some ache in the abdomen. Slowly it turned worse. He had to move to the civil hospital. After a few hours he passed away. The family has almost turned mad."

Pona Dada had died. He was just forty five years old. Almost a young man. He had been suffering from gastric for a long time. He didn't get married as he had no job. Yet, he toiled in the field whole day long. How would he manage the food if he did not work? Although their age did not match yet Bikash developed a close friendship with Pona Dada. It's not because they belonged to the same clan but because they had certain aspects in similar. Both of them did not slander. Whenever he thought of slandering an incident came to Bikash's mind.

The only job for the jobless housewives for the whole day long was slandering. In the process, at times, they were entangled in heated arguments also. Whenever Bikash noticed all these he felt pity for them. At times he was angry on them and sometimes he laughed at them. Bikash had a very bad experience regarding slandering. Pona Dada didn't possess this habit at all. He had been very straightforward in his comments regarding other people. So, the news of Pona Dada's death had startled Bikash a bit . Bikash was contemplating whether he would go to Pona Dada's house or not.

Amaiya once again said, "There is another sad news for you. You might be hurt if I don't let you know now. But don't rush there now. If you want to you may visit tomorrow morning. They might have slept by now".

"What happened?" asked Bikash curiously.

"Hara **Daiti** died too."

"What? Hara **Daiti** too died."

"Yes!"

Bikash's head started spinning. Hara **Daiti** was a good friend of his. Hara **Daiti** was almost thirty-five years older than Bikash. His younger son was of Bikash's age. In the whole village, if Bikash had any intimate friend it was Hara **Daiti**. There was a reason behind their friendship. Since childhood Bikash had seen Hara **Daiti** in their house. He went to his house only to sleep. Hara **Daiti** did not possess any land. He worked as a shared farmer. He had his own land once. But whenever necessity came he sold some of it and had given mortgage for money which left him landless. Hara Diati had four sons and five daughters. His elder son was of Pona Dada's age and had got five kids himself. Hara **Daiti** could only marry off a daughter. Everyone else chose for themselves. One of his son was in jail for theft. Others worked as labourers. His eldest son was a shared farmer like Hara **Daiti** himself. Hara **Daiti** had never seen a glint of happiness in his life. Yet, no one had ever witnessed a glint of sadness in his face. He always laughed in some or other pretext. During his school days they passed maximum time together except the school hours. While Bikash was studying he sat on the floor beside his table quietly.

Bikash's mother shouted, "Hara **Kai**, come out from there. He is studying. Hara **Daiti** replied instantly, "I am not disturbing your son. I am just sitting here." **Daiti** did not get up. Hara **Daiti** never got angry. Bikash read the newspaper to him. At times **Daiti** commented in between. Sometimes Bikash read to him one or two stories from books. He read the story of **Macbeth** to him translating into Assamese. Diati got angry on Lady Macbeth. Bikash did not understand why **Daiti** was never sad!

"**Daiti**, have you taken lunch?"

"Wherefrom I would manage lunch son, don't have rice."

"What? You have not taken lunch?"

"In fact I have not eaten anything since last noon. It does not matter. My wife was shouting at me, I could not tolerate. So, I had my bath and came out. Don't you have school today? "

"Today is a holiday for Buddha Purnima."

"Oh Yes! Look how forgetful I have turned. I haven't ploughed today only because it's a full moon. Well, since I haven't taken anything today it can be termed as fasting on occasion of full moon."

Bikash didn't understand how could Hara **Daiti** joke about his starvation so easily. **Daiti** had some other qualities too.

"**Daiti**, take lemon with lentil. It's very tasty."

"It needs not to be mentioned. Any kind of sour item makes the lentil tasty."

If someone else said, "But **Daiti**, its bitter to have lentil with a bit of chilly."

"Oh yes! It's very tasty to have lentil with a bit of chilly."

"No, Hara **Kai**, it's better to have lentil without adding anything"

"You are right. It's better to have lentil without adding anything."

"**Daiti**, that elder son of Rameswar has gone astray."

"You are correct! Rameswar's elder son has totally gone astray. I have been noticing it for many days."

"**Daiti** I don't agree with others. Rameswar's elder son is a very good boy. He is very honest."

"I totally agree with you. Rameswar's elder son is the best. I have been noticing him since his childhood."

The same Hara **Daiti** had died. Bikash could not believe. As if Hara **Daiti** couldn't have died. All the events of Hara **Daiti**'s life had started coming to his mind the moment he had heard the news about his death. If environment made man then what environment was responsible for making Hara **Daiti** like this? Sometime he sat to eat after skipping two meals. Suddenly a beggar came there praying for alms. He gave half of the food from his plate to the beggar. Another day he took some bananas to the market to sell. On the way some small children shouted, "Grandpa, please give us some bananas."

"But son, I have to sell them. Otherwise, I have to stay in darkness because I don't have oil to light the lamp." Saying this he proceeded. But if they lingered still, he would give them half of the bananas. The other half he took to the market and if he could not sell them, he brought it back home. That's why everyone liked **Daiti**. People took advantage from him. If they saw some good fruit in **Daiti**'s orchard, the brahmin from his neighborhood came to his house and said, "Hara **Kai**, will the bananas of your orchard be ripped by next full moon?"

"It might, Why do you ask?"

"Actually we promised a **Saitseva** before our middle son got the job. We planned to offer the puja with the money of his first salary. But it has been three months now. My wife is imploring me to offer the puja soon and has informed me about the bananas in your orchard. I want to offer the puja in this monsoon. If you think it will be ripe by then, kindly cut it from the tree and put it on the slab over the fire place. "

"Don't you worry? I shall cut it before lunch."

"But how much money do you need for this?"

"You want to offer the bananas in **Saitseva**, don't you? Why would I take money from your Prabhu? "

"That's true. One should offer something to Saitseva if he can. Still you are a needy man."

"Say no more **Prabhu**! I won't be a rich man by selling the bananas to you for **Saitseva**. My need will be fulfilled by His blessings. You can take it. I shall take it to your house."

"Hara, haven't you ploughed the land today?"

"No."

"What will you do the whole day then?"

"The day will pass somehow."

"Why don't you come to our house then? You can have some tea and help me in repairing the fence."

"You just go ahead. I am coming with the **Dao**."

When Bikash passed the matriculation Hara **Daiti** said, "Saru pona, you have passed matric. Now you will be a judge. Will you remember me after that also?"

"That's true, when I will become a judge I will think of bigger matters. How would Hara **Daiti** be remembered then? Where will there be time to remember **Daiti**? "

"True, true; when you will become a judge you will be very busy. You won't be able to think about us even if you want to."

"Who said I won't have any time **Daiti**? Don't judges think about human beings?"

"That's true! Judge must think about human beings."

Bikash could not sleep. The whole night thoughts of both Pona Dada and Hara **Daiti** had created uproar in his mind. His friendship with Hara **Daiti** existed even after he had reached college. In holidays whenever he came home, he went to Hara **Daiti** first. After getting a job, once Bikash gave Hara **Daiti** ten rupees. He did not take it.

In the morning after taking tea Bikash first visited Pona Dada's house and later he visited Hara **Daiti**'s house. The three sons of Hara **Daiti** were there at home. Hara **Daiti**'s elder son had described Bikash the condition of their father before death. Before two months of his death the doctor advised them to take him to Barbari. But they couldn't manage the fare to go there. Hara **Daiti** himself resisted to the idea. He would have been saved if he would have been taken to Barbari. During his last days, he could not eat anything. He asked for Bikash frequently. Bikash's eyes became moist. Finally, he stood up.

The elder son accompanied Bikash to the gate. With them came the seven-year-old kids of his. Near the gate the elder sons said to Bikash,

"Soru pona if you don't mind, I want to tell you something." Bikash had said, "Please, feel free to say anything." "Father wanted to eat rohu fish a few days before he died. But I could not manage even a single piece. Now I am thinking of giving rohu fish in the last feast given in respect of the dead. If you pay me the cost of a kilogram of rohu fish, I will be able to fulfill the last wish of my father."

Bikash turned speechless. The grandchildren of Hara **Daiti** who were standing near him started whispering, "That day Prakash brought scales of rohu fish. I exchanged a scale with two seeds. "Do you want to have a look?" He ran home and brought the scale. Prakash always ate rohu fish in their home. His father was an Inspector."

"Do you know I have seen rohu fish?" The sister said.

"Don't bluff."

Wait, I will show it to you. She ran into the house. She brought her book and had started to turn the pages. She shouted to her brother, "Look, this is rohu."

Both the kids started looking at the picture. The scale of the rohu fish was still in the elder brother's hand.

Bikash started moving with fast steps. The faster he walked, the more the sound of the word 'rohu' started beating in his ears.

Sorrow of Love

On the forehead of the young girl there was a vermilion mark of white sandalwood. There was now a way to confirm her status as a widow as there was no child marriage these days. If child marriage would have existed, then a young girl of twenty five or twenty six could have been a widow. The face was a nice sculpture like a statue. Looking at her round reddish face and blackish eyes, one was reminded of two bumblebees struck on a lotus flower. She was wearing a white saree that looked like shewali flower. She was not wearing any ornament either in her ear or in her neck, nor in her hands. She worked in a bookstore and kept on reading either a newspaper or a book when there was no customer. Both the items were available in her shop. One could not easily guess whether she was a worker there or owner of the shop because another pale-faced girl sat there without any visible enthusiasm. It was difficult to fathom who helped whom. The book stall named "Puthighar" had a good stock of newspaper, books, papers, pens, etc.

Having been transferred from the post of cooperative officer, the writer looked at the shop at the first instant as he was coming out of the circuit house in a rickshaw in order to join the new office. It was quite natural that his eyes attracted the attention of the shop as it was his habit to look out for a bookshop whenever he was transferred.

As his eyes roamed around he marked the bookshop called "Puthighar" situated at the cross road. At the same time his gaze fixed on the girl who was sitting in the shop. He was passing the shop on a rickshaw.

While returning from his office, Upamanyu Baruah got down from the rickshaw near "Puthighar" as the circuit house was nearer. Entering the shop, he enquired if there was any newspaper or not.

Only two newspapers were there. The voice of the girl seemed like the tune that came out of the strings of a sitar. Such a melodious tone, screen and composed.

"—— Give me those two newspapers. Is there any magazine here? I have not been able to look at any magazines or periodicals during the last ten days." When he finished the girl handed him over a few magazines. Upamanyu was a writer and being curious, he felt like asking a few questions to the girl. It seemed that her beautiful and composed appearance had given birth to many tales of many books.

"Are you the owner of the shop?"

"Yes I am."

"And what about the land?"

" It's rented."

Every word of the girl seemed to be deep and transparent as though some one was dropping pebbles on a jar full of water.

Upamanyu looked at the girl and informed her that he had been newly transferred there. She expanded the gaze of her open eyes and looked at Upamanyu like the gaze of a dear. He felt a bit embarrassed even though he was aged. Naming a few newspapers, Upamanyu came out of the shop. The girl did not speak at all. But the girl kept on looking at him with her wide open eyes till he was visible on the road. Did not he feel embarrassed at all? But ideally he did not feel embarrassed at all as the girl was like his own daughter who was pursuing her studies to become a doctor. Like her own daughter, Upamanyu was a humorous person. He kept on cracking jokes with his lover or his wife. His wife who happened to be a lecturer pulled his legs while he came.

"Look, don't make love with other women, pretending to be a bachelor."

"Do you know my age? I am fifty two-years-old. Earlier, a fifty two years man was considered an old person but nowadays one is regarded a senior citizen at sixty."

"A man is never judged by his age, You are a writer, you look handsome and your hair has not yet turned grey. So why do you worry?"

Otherwise he would have pulled his wife's legs over the telephone regarding this girl but he decided not to crack jokes as the girl was like a lotus flower with a considerably serious personality. It would be an injustice.

Gradually, Upamanyu felt that he must see the girl while going to the office around nine or nine thirty in the morning. Otherwise he would feel like leaving aside something. He would feel depressed. Why should it be like that? He was not a weak or fragile person. He had developed a fatherly affection for the girl like his own daughter. But he had not yet come across such a girl having such serious demeanor. And apart from all these, she was so beautiful. One day the girl abruptly asked Upamanyu, "Sir, can I ask you a question?"

"Please do ask. Don't mind as I am addressing you with dearest terms."

Addressing him with respect she pulled out a book from his bag and pointing at the passport size photograph on the back cover asked, "Aren't you the same person?".

"Yes I am. But don't reveal my identity to others. Because I don't want to be invited to meetings like writers and politicians as they are much revered in Assam. I don't like to attend meetings. I have not disclosed my identity even in office. I am fortunate that service men here don't keep abreast of the latest books and magazines. Now I want to ask you, "What's your name?"

"Ulupi."

"What is your educational qualification?"

"I completed my M.A."

"Do you belong to this locality?"

"Yes, I do. I live nearer to your office, about one kilometer away from here. Where do you stay Sir?"

"In circuit house. I shall not take a rented room as I have come here for only two months. Okay you stay here. "

"Please comply with my request. Do not disclose my identity to others."

Upamanyu came out of the shop and looked back after reaching the main road. No, the girl was not looking at him. She was rather looking at the bag she was carrying in her hand.

Upamanyu felt like asking many a question to Ulupi. But her respectfulness and seriousness were discouraging him to ask her any further questions.

"Who else is there at your home?"

"Father has expired. Only my mother is there along with two brothers." Having given him this bit of information she looked at the road. He looked at the newspaper in his hand and enquired,

"When did your father expire?"

"Six years back."

"What had happened to him?"

"Father went to Sonari. There was a bomb in the bus."

Ulupi informed that three persons died in the bomb blast and she was quite dispassionate. His attitude seemed to be quite casual to Upamanyu. Upamanyu looked at Ulupi as she stooped down. Her hair was dense and black like a bee. Upamanyu shifted away his glance as his roving eyes fixed on the face of the pale-faced girl.

"Is she your relative?"

"She is like my sister, Sir. She lives nearby."

"Okay you stay here." He said that as he came out of the office quite late today. He was coming out of the shop carrying the newspaper in his hand. At that precise moment Ulupi called him.

"Do you want to tell anything?"

"It's almost two months. We have not yet talked properly."

"Why do you say so? I always keep on talking to you. And I have also let you know that you are very close to me."

"Tomorrow is a holiday. Will you be at the circuit house?"

"Yes, I will be there.."

"Sir, is it okay, if I go there around 10 a.m.? He was surprised by Ulupi's words. The beautiful young girl did not talk so much. She only replied to inquire of Upamanyu. "

He felt quite surprised as she expressed her wish to meet him alone. Devoid of her father, would she ask for a job? Thinking this, he felt a bit helpless.

"No, there will be no problem. You can surely come."

What would the girl say? Her face and eyes were laced with a tinge of sadness. Her tone revealed a sad line. What would she – a young and beautiful girl tell a candid story writer like him? When he first saw her, she turned out to be a mysterious girl for him. He felt like asking many questions to her. But he did not dare to do so even though he was acclaimed as an angry writer by many critics. But now it was quite strange that a girl was daring enough to ask him something which may not be to his likings. But would she talk about herself or about others? Maybe she would talk about her father who died in the bomb blast engineered by the extremist? He also died a premature death. His father happened to be a teacher and opened this bookshop. It was looked after by a boy in the morning and by her father in the evening. Would she talk about her father then who died in the bomb blast.

He suffered from insomnia and he felt disturbed regarding the matter. He could not sleep till late night. He also contemplated the possibility of venturing out to the residence of the girl. What was strange that he had joined this government office for just two months and he had now passed one and half months but still the other workers of his office did not know his identity as a writer. Ulupi also did not betray his trust.

If she would have disclosed his real identity then she could have easily sold his books available at the shop. His co-workers in the office would have bought many of his books in order to appease him and they could have also flattered him a lot. He was surprised to find out that a girl was capable of digesting a secret. And now this same mysterious girl would meet him at 10.00 a.m. in order to talk.

The sound of the calling bell forced him to look at the watch – yes it was 10'o clock. It must be Ulupi and he was again surprised to find such punctuality in case of an Assamese girl. His wife who was above fifty years of age took a lot of time while coming from his room to the courtyard where the car was parked. He kept on blowing the horn and yet she was always late. A lecturer took such a long time but a young unmarried girl came so readily. This then added importance to the girl in the mind of the writer. He opened the door and invited her to come inside. She came inside and sat on the sofa. She obliged.

"Have you closed the bookshop?"

"There is no one on holidays. The customers come to take the newspapers and apart from that the other girl is there."

"What relation do you share with the girl?"

"She is like my sister." Having said this, Ulupi looked at the table in front of her. The writer was at unease. As a matter of fact he closed the door when the girl came inside. Circuit House. It may auger trouble. But it would diminish the dignity of the girl if the door was opened now. Intelligently he eked out a way. He went outside with a jar, fetched water and came back with the filled jar and this time he kept the door open. Rather the door was half open this time as a sign of carelessness.

" Sir, it really gives me immense pleasure to read your books."

"I thought so when I saw many of my books in your shop."

"The readers like you because in spite of being a government officer you always chronicle the truth with courage in your writing."

He did not make any comments after Ulupi's remarks.

Other writers who liked publicity would have used this chance. They would have valorized themselves in front of the girl and also praised their courage for the depiction of the truth. There was no dearth of writers who beat their own trumpets. Though Upamanyu did not even utter a single word but he was quite surprised to find out that a girl liked his bold and straightforward writing. But he decided against it.

"Sir, I came to talk to you. Do you have any urgent work?"

"No, its okay. I do not have any work right now. Today, I do not even have writing assignment. I wrote a few articles for the next week yesterday and sent those."

"Sir, can I start? She spoke raising her pupil wide eyes."

"Yes, please do."

"I may be garrulous. If you find it boring kindly tell me. I won't mind. Many people do not like to hear other peoples' personal life. "

"No, I don't mind. Please open your heart." He wanted to tell that a story writer never disliked to hear other peoples' secret, but he thought that probably the girl might take it otherwise. So, he decided against it. He was suddenly reminded of a couplet by Khojal Kanpuri.

"Hume to mauji totatum ka taskira hai pasand. O aur hai jo kinaro ki baat karte hai."

The Assamese translation also surfaced in his mind immediately. **"I like to describe the aggressive wind of the storm. It is not possible to speak only of the bank."**

"Sir, I want to speak about a girl."

"Please start."

"If I narrate with leisure then it would also be difficult for me. If I summarize, you can figure it out because you are an intelligent writer. You can understand. She halted for a few seconds as she kept on touching the pen on the table like a coy girl."

"Sir, the girl belongs to a middle class family. She is good at studies. She never failed. Rather she always secured either first division or second division. While she was in the ninth standard she came into contact with a boy of Higher Secondary."

"Actually, one develops infatuation instead of love at that age. The boy had many qualities. Good at studies, a tall handsome young man, he was equally good at sports and he dexterously played the flute. From the higher secondary till the completion of his graduation he always secured the first position in the flute playing competition. His father was a clerk at the S.D.C office. But according to his family members he was a misfit in the contemporary world as he did not take any bribe from anyone." Having told all these, Ulupi halted for a few moments. The writer who was listening to everything so carefully offered her a glass of water quite stealthily. She gave the impression of being thirsty as she gulped the water.

"Do you want another glass of water?"

"No sir, its okay. I doubted whether you are getting bored."

"No, No, please don't think like that. You met me on the very day I came to this locality. We know each other. You are an educated and intelligent girl. Can't you figure out what sort of person I am?"

"Still sir, you are famous and busy at the same time. Gradually the boy and the girl fell in love. The boy's father retired. The girl had two elder sisters and one younger sister. The boy secured second class fifth position in Mathematics in B.Sc. He could not pursue M.Sc. Even his father who was a stern and honest person had to bribe in order to draw money after retirement. In spite of that he only got half the amount, the remaining amount was released by his family members after his death."

"Is the boy engaged in any job?"

"No, he does not. You know how hard contemporary life is."

"What do you mean? "

"One gets job if only one can bribe. Where will he get the money?"

"What about the elder sister of the boy?"

"No, sir they are also jobless. One does tuition while the other is ill. She is suffering from asthma. The other sister works in our shop."

"Didn't she get married?"

"She belongs to a poor family."

"You are right, many boys want girls with jobs these days."

"Did the boy sincerely look for a job? "

"The boy literally looked everywhere for a job."

"His efforts were salutary. Yet, he failed."

"The Assamese boy gave more importance to jobs ..."

"No sir, Ulupi snatched his words – he even tried his hand in business. In order to get loan from the bank one has to bribe. One of his friends had to bribe one and half lakh to get the job of industry officer. But the officer was the son of their ideal teacher."

"Didn't he get loan?"

"No sir, he did not. What happened afterwards?"

"He met the same fortune that is the lot of militants. He didn't tell anyone. He didn't even tell his beloved. Just dropped a letter. The entire house was full of hue and cry. "

" What is more is that the house was raided by police and military. They kept on tormenting the family members. And then Sir one day....Ulupi compassed herself."

She gave the feeling of being embarrassed or reluctant.

"What happened?"

There was a knock on the door of the boy's house.

Probably the boy came.

The parents thought like that. Someone was knocking at the door and speaking something in whispers. It was also raining. When the aged person opened the door he was literally dragged out and then there was a sound of revolver. After that there was a strange silence. After sometime the door opened. Nothing could be visible as there was no light. When a candle light was brought, the blood soaked dead body of the old man came into view. The boy's father was killed.

"Who killed him?"

"The secret killers."

"Why did they kill the old man?"

"Because his son was an extremist..." Having said this Ulupi looked at the sky through the open window. Sitting at the bunch of a Kanchan flower, a crow was making shrill noise. Suddenly she cried out as though something was passing through her veins. The scenario was really awful.

"He used to write letters to the girl," Ulupi said, as she kept on looking outside. And what about the girl?

"She also writes letters till today."

"Now what problem does the girl face? Kindly let me know what is actually her problem."

Everybody was forcing the girl to get married. Every one close to her was taking utmost care to convince her to get married soon. They were not only pressuring her, they were also making her life miserable.

"What is her age?"

"She is thirty two years old."

"It's natural then that her near and dear ones would pressurize her to get married. But what is her view?"

"Sir, she would get married only to her lover, that boy who has joined the extremists."

"She can never get married to anyone else. Even if she dies, she would marry only that boy. The family members are pursuing her towards separation and any other girl would have been tempted to commit suicide under such circumstances."

Both of them fell silent for some time. Ulupi again looked through the open window with her wide open eyes and then she looked at Upamanyu before playing with the ball pen again. A suspicion surfaced in Upamanyu's mind. This very girl who was sitting in front of him and narrating the sad tale of a girl – was she herself the protagonist of the tale? Even though some girls were structurally weak still they were fit enough. Their age also seemed less. Even though Ulupi looked like a girl of about twenty five years, she would be around thirty one or thirty two. He might be right. He felt like asking this question to the girl who was sitting in front of him.. If he asked the question, would it be humiliating to the girl as she had not uttered the name of the girl yet and also gave the impression that she was narrating the life of someone else. If he asked with the right intention it would be humiliating but what would happen if she took it as humiliation.

Would not she be hurt? She was a serious girl and also had a robust personality. The writer also felt like the girl's father. She had narrated this tale with profound respect and intense faith. She had just known the writer for a few days, yet she had trusted him who was otherwise a male. That is why he would not betray her trust. Would she mind? He looked at her. She again looked through the window and marked the crow sitting on the bunch of Kanchan flowers. Anyone could fathom that her eyes were fixed on the tree but actually she did not particularly look at anything. It was like an album of old memories, the pages of which kept on opening one by one. It was as though her gaze was fixed on that.

"Can I ask you a question?"

She looked at him like a red dear but did not raise her eyes.

"I want to ask you a question but was granted permission by a marginal movement of the head. Even though she gave the permission, he felt reluctant. Even though he was acclaimed as a courageous writer he was quite shaky to ask her any question. Wasn't he afraid? Should he be afraid of her?"

"Would I be wrong if I guess that you and the girl whose tale you narrated are identical?"

Now, he directly looked at the face of the girl. She was also looking at him with still eyes. And he suddenly marked that tears were rolling down the cheeks of the girl. Seeing the tear drops on her face he felt a bit embarrassed. If he would have known earlier, he would not have caused pain to her. One can never take back ones comment like a gun fire that comes out once.

"Was I right in my guess?" Upamanyu asked this looking at her courageously.

Ulupi silently looked at him for a few seconds and without closing her eyes told with a deep voice, "Yes, I am that girl."

Ulupi's eyes kept on blinking like a wet marble in water. And her words struck a deep chord in the heart of the writer "Yes I am, Yes I am." He looked for a few seconds at the still eyes of Ulupi. No, he could not look, He shifted his glance. He felt helpless. As though this girl had pointed a picture of despondency in his heart.

"Sir, can't you write a story. I shall get mental peace."

Ulupi looked at the writer with her bumblebee like eyes which was also tearful.

"And everybody would realize then. Nobody would disturb me."

"Okay. I shall write the story, But what is the problem if you get married? Don't your family members allow you to get married to him." Having said this he looked at Ulupi with courage.

"But whom would I marry?"

"With your lover. What is his name?"

"Prasenjeet."

"So, can't you get married to Prasenjeet? Won't he marry you?"

"We made a resolve twelve years back, We can't marry any one apart from each other."

Since you have waited for so long, so please wait for a few more days. He would surely come back one day. Your love is profound ... Upamanyu halted at this point. He silently looked at Ulupi. Looking at his face, Ulupi suddenly unzipped her bag. She brought out a folded newspaper and placed it in front of Upamanyu. There was a colourful photograph on the very first page of the newspaper. A photograph of a blood soaked young boy. One side of the head had smashed.

"Who is he?"

"He is Prasenjeet Sir, he is none other than Prasenjeet." Having uttered these words, Ulupi was trembling like a railway train passing through a long bridge. Gradually the girl leaned on the sitting chair. Would she tumble down now?

The Coy Fisher Girl

Ila was a good girl. Although she belonged to the fisherman community, she was neat and clean. She wore the same frock, yet it was clean. The frock was colorful. The white petals of the red flower of her frock remained white. People would think that she had seven same frocks and everyday she wore one. But in reality it was not the fact, she had just one frock. According to her parents she loved to stay neat and clean from her childhood. Sometimes her mother scolded her, "Being a fisher girl, why are you so fashionable?" Whenever she told her father to bring soap for her, he looked at the coins in his pocket and remembered that he had to buy tobacco and paper. He went out coughing and after coming back he brought out the tobacco and paper from his pocket and said, "Ila dear, I couldn't manage to buy soap for you today. If possible tomorrow I shall buy you one." Earlier she grumbled whenever her father answered her like that. Her bedridden mother Bohagi shouted at her, "Do you think yourself to be a princess that you need a piece of soap daily? No prince is coming for you." Ila kept quite. She was intelligent. One day after school she had asked Pramila **Baideu**, "Baideu, it is written in General Knowledge books that one can wash clothes with the ashes of dry banana leaf. How it can be done? Pramila Baideu thought for some time. She also had read and learned it but she didn't have any practical idea about it. That day she had left promising her to explain the matter the next day. She had kept her promise. Ila had started washing clothes in the same manner. This has saved her from mother's scolding and father's indifference.

Her mother always scolded. They were six brothers and sisters including Ila. Ila was the eldest of all. Ila had come to a conclusion that bedridden people scolded their children more. Like her mother many women in the neighborhood were bedridden and strangely enough all of them kept on scolding their children from bed. After her recovery, Khudumai's mother beat them even in the minutest of opportunity. That day she beat Khudumai so cruely that Khudumai had prepared to jump in the water in sadness. Luckily Ila met her on the way. In tears Khudumai uttered, "If the flood washes away our huts this time I will be very happy. I want to see the bastard dead. But Ila could never think like her, neither in reality nor in dreams. Even in her bedridden condition her mother gave birth to a child every year. Khudu's mother also went through the same condition. Blasphemy is a sin otherwise Ila would have entered the **Naamghar** and expressed her resentment against God. No puja had ever done any good. Her mother, Khudu's mother, Rameswar's father, Kameswar's elder brother, Barlora's grandmother - all of these were bedridden for ages. A **Gossain** named Jadu Kabiraj came twice in a year. He tried to treat them by incantation and gave them a charmed amulet. For these they had to pay the **Gossain** both in cash and kind. The **Gossain** cooked for himself.

One day Ila went to **Naamghar**. Her mother sent her to bring medicine from the **Gossain**. When she reached the **Gossain** was sleeping. The person who helped the **Gossain** was also sleeping. It started to drizzle. In the fence outside clothes were put to dry. As a habit, Ila brought the clothes in carefully and put it on a mat. She sat on another mat. The **Gossain** woke up at the sound of the thundering. He looked at her with dissatisfaction. Ila felt frightened. The **Gossain** asked in his gruff voice. "Who are you?" Ila had told in a shivering voice," I am Krishna Das's daughter." " Who has brought these clothes ?" " I have, otherwise, it would have got wet." Her words made the **Gossain** angry. In a rough voice he told her, "How dare a fisher girl like you sit in front of me. Get up from that mat at once". Deukan, Deukan – "Pravu." Deukan, his helper came responding to the **Gossain**. The **Gossain** said, "Look, what the girl has done? She has touched all the dry clothes. Go and wash them again. And you….." By this time Ila had risen from the mat "Wash the mat." Deukon too scolded Ila. Ila grabbed the mat and came out. It was raining outside. She threw the mat in the rain and ran out. Ila stopped in Mathura's shop. She thought what her fault might be. She belonged to the fisherman community. But Runu too belonged to the same community. The **Gossain** visited Runu's house. He travelled in Runu's father's cars. He even took whatever Runu served. But when she had touched those dry clothes they had be to washed again! She did not understand this behavior. She did not bring the medicine. Was it really a medicine she wondered. He would give some incanted water. It had to be taken without spilling a drop on earth. Her mother had taken a lot of such medicine and amulets. But her condition had not improved a bit during these three years. Her mother would again scold her today. Her parents caught fish in the river earlier. Those fish were sold in the market. They didn't catch fish nowadays. Her mother was bedridden. Her father was suffering from cough. He couldn't go in the water. While taking boiled rice and papaya in lunch, Ila remembered their bygone days. Her siblings cried. Her mother scolded them from bed. Ila kept quite.

Ila was a good girl . Till the first standard she studied in the private Primary School of their neighbourhood started by Premada **Mastarni** in the **Naamghar**. After passing the first standard she had to be shifted to another school where she could study till third standard. The parents didn't want her to study any further. She needed to take care of the siblings since her mother was ill. Ila had started crying.

As Ila was good in studies, when Premada **Mastarni** got to know about the situation, she took the responsibility of buying books and clothes for Ila. One day Ila's father had taken her to the Lower Primary School which was one and half mile away from their home. Admitting her in the school Ila's father said to the Headmaster, "Master, I have admitted her only because of her persistence. Actually children from our community shouldn't be studying. Both her mother and I are ill too. We need someone to look after the children. Please excuse her if she is absent sometimes." Dangar Mai alias Ila was a good girl. She always came to school. At times she was late. The colour of her skin was fair.

There were fifty students in the whole class. Among them Ila was the brightest. But she was always sullen. The Headmaster and Ramen master had noticed it. She was good in studies, yet she was so cheerless. Ramen master tried to make her laugh. She couldn't laugh, she didn't. She was ten-years-old. The Headmaster sometimes scolded her for being so cheerless. She couldn't cry too. Just two drops of water rolled down from her eyes like a dying stream.

.The Headmaster loved her. During recess he gave her to boil tea for the teachers and gave her to drink too. When she poured tea for the Headmaster she remembered Jadu Kabiraj **Gossain**. She had to wash the mat that day. The Headmaster was also a **Gossain** like him. She learnt to calculate average. So in her calculation this kind of people were found only one per cent. There was no use of just being one among hundred.

Ila was a sharp girl. She had secured first position while getting promoted from second standard to third standard. Ramen master had brought her books, copies, etc. The Headmaster had presented her a fountain pen. Her old frock had suffered uncountable number of stitches. The Headmaster had brought her a new frock. She accepted the gift with hesitation. Tears rolled down over her cheeks. She had wanted to touch the Headmaster's feet. He had stopped her half way and had uttered, "Study well. You have to get scholarship."

After remaining absent for almost two months, one day Ila came to school. She didn't have any book with her. She went to the Headmaster and said, "Sir I will not be able to come to school anymore. My mother died." All the teachers including the Headmaster had advised her to come to school. She came now and then. She did not talk to anyone. One of her teachers had also insulted her for being so quiet. Still she kept quite. At times she brought her two and half years old sister too. After one hour or so her sister started crying. Taking her books and the sister along she left the school. Though silent, tears fell from her eyes too. After she left, the teachers of the school discussed about her. The school was situated beside the river. Most of the students belonged either to fishermen community, miri community or cobbler community.Their condition was almost similar. But everyone didn't get noticed. But Ila did. It's because she was a good girl, she was a smart girl. She was neat and clean. The teachers discussed, but they couldn't do anything. Ila had stopped coming to school.

The Headmaster sent her a message to come to school. She had to appear in the examination anyhow. She had to secure first position in the whole district.

She came on the day of the examination. When the result came out it was seen that she had again secured first position. But her marks had decreased. Ramen Master had asked her a few questions which she couldn't reply. Previously, she had answered these questions properly. But what had happened to her now? Ila had forgot everything. If she didn't improve, she would not be able to get scholarship save standing first in the whole district.

Every year they taught those students who would appear in the scholarship examination for two months. This year also it would take place. This year Ila would have to be properly taken care of. She had the capability of securing first position in the whole district. Ila was sharp. Her handwriting was more beautiful than the printed letters.

The Headmaster again landed in trouble as Ila had stopped coming to school after the results. He had sent messages many a time. Still she did not appear. One day, Raman master and the Headmaster himself had gone to her village after the school to search for her. It was stinky everywhere. There was nothing like gateway in the houses. There were heaps of garbage and cow dung, etc in front of the houses. There was not a proper house in the village. A few naked children had surrounded them. A three feet broad passage was used as road. Someone was scolding the other. In some homes, the whole family was busy in work. Everyone was wearing the most necessary clothes. There was a great similarity between the clothes of the male and the female. It was in the colour of their clothes. Both the Headmaster and Ramen master didn't know the name of Ila's father. They had asked one girl. "Do you know which one is Ila's house? She couldn't reply. They only knew Dangar Mai not Ila. Suddenly, Ramen master remembered her nickname. They had asked about Dangar Mai's house. The girl pointed out. Both of them entered the yard. A bunch of kids were playing in the yard. A child was crying sitting on the verandah. Someone was coughing inside.

The Headmaster had asked, "Is Dangar Mai at home?"

"No," came the reply.

"Where is she?" Ramen asked.

"No one knows. She has gone early in the morning. Every day she goes."

The Headmaster peeped in through the door - a fire was burning on the floor. Near the fire there was a bed. A man was sleeping on it. He couldn't gather courage to call the man. "Tell her to come to school tomorrow. Tell her that Head Sir and Ramen Sir came. "

But Ila didn't come to school even on the next day. He had sent her messages to come to school anyhow. This time Ila came.

The school broke. The Headmaster and Ramen master came out to go home. Ila was standing near the tube well. Her frock was dirty. She was holding the rim of her frock between her thigh. They came near her. The Headmaster asked, "Where have you been all these days?" She kept quiet. Ramen said, "We have been searching for you. Why didn't you come to school? Do you know how many days are left for examination?" Ila couldn't utter a word. She was shivering. The Headmaster asked, "where do you go everyday?" She still kept quiet. With a rough voice the Headmaster uttered again, "why didn't you come yesterday?" She said shivering, "Sir, I don't have pants." Uttering this she pressed the rim of her frock between her thigh with her hands.

"Don't you have pants? Are you wearing one now?"

"No", saying this she started sobbing looking at the Headmaster.

Ila was a good girl. She was holding her frock between her thigh tight, otherwise it would get lifted by the wind.

Glossary

Baideu: An endearing term used to address an elderly respected lady.

Naamghar: A traditional prayer house of the Assamese people.

Gossain: A respected person occupying a place of dignity in Sattra

Masterni: A typical rural expression to address a female teacher.

Master: A typical rural expression to address a male teacher.

The Naked Weaver

Paragpawan, Apurba and Hafiz were standing in the yard and looking around. There was silence everywhere. The sun was on the zenith. They thought that there was no one inside the hut. The narrow, small road leading to the hut was so bumpy that they had to park both of their scooters near the shop in the juncture. A few naked children circled around the scooters. The shopkeeper Pramod tried to shoo them away like animals. It was Pramod's idea to park the scooters there and walk down the one and half furlong distance. After walking for some time they had realized that Pramod had given a very practical idea. Otherwise, they would have skidded off the road. Paragpawan who had some leftist leanings blurted out in anger, "In the 50th year of independence just look at the condition of our village roads. Can you call it a road? Never mind the people. Had those people who wanted to build a golden Assam ever walked on these roads? They should be dragged over these roads, damn it."

Apurba and Hafiz kept mum because they helped the existing government in elections although they had lost faith in them now. If they tried to defend themselves, sharp-tongued Paragpawan would not let them go away. So, they kept quiet.

Standing on the yard they could not guess if there was someone inside the house or not. There was silence everywhere. The bamboo door of the hut was ajar. On the top of the roof, pigeons were cooing from its nest. This gave the surroundings a grave aura. Apurba looked at his watch - It's twelve past twenty five. No one was there in the neighbor's yard also. Hafiz noticed a red-colored dog was sleeping in a corner of the verandah. He glanced at them once and folded himself in again.

"Is anyone home? Is anyone home?" They called twice from outside and were looking at the door expecting somebody to come out. But there was no movement.

"Is anyone home? We have come from Jorhat."

They heard a groan inside the hut. It's a female voice telling someone about the guests outside. They felt relieved. Someone was inside. A little later a man came out wearing a yellowish dhoti and a gamosa hanging over his shoulder. Seeing the man the dog sleeping in the corner of the verandah came near him and started shaking its tail. They had noticed that the man looked like a skeleton wrapped in skin as if a **Navapatrika** wrapped in a saree near the Durga idol. The tall skeleton-like man rubbed the dust from the bench and chair and said, "have a seat."

All three sat on the small bench. On the walls a few photos were hanging which were covered with dust. The skeleton-like man sat on a there-legged stool and looked at them.

"We have come from Jorhat. Is it not the house of Rangai Oja?"

The skeleton-like man nodded.

"How many people are there in your house?" Paragpawan asked.

"Only the old woman."

"And, no one else?"

'No', said the man and let out a deep sigh. Suddenly they realized that the question should not have been asked.

'No one at all' , Paragpawan asked the man with blurred eyes.

"With much difficulty we had a boy and a girl after ten years of our marriage. The boy came two years after the girl was born."

"And," Hafiz asked.

"Both of them grew up." The man abruptly stopped and gazed at their eyes.

"What's your purpose for coming here?" The question brought them back to the real world.

"Like previous years, this year also we are going to organize a **Bihu** function in the Kachari field."

Rangai Oja didn't pay much attention to their words and looked through the open door with an absent face. Hafiz felt puzzled. But a different question hovered around in Paragpawan's mind. What might have happened to the children? But he could not gather courage to ask the question.

Paragpawan was the person who first proposed to invite Rangai Oja. Everyone else wanted to invite dramatist, director and trainer, Habibur Rahman. Paragpawan opposed the proposal. He couldn't resist himself and started shouting, "Why should that womanizer be invited for such kind of responsibility? He has some private drummers who perform for him. Have you read his dramas? He has copied from Ritwik Ghatak to N. Frank. It's easy to get popularity in Assam. Do you know what happens in his training? He plays cassette and teaches dancing.."

There was no point of criticizing somebody's character so harshly in public. And what made you so angry when he mentioned Habibur Rahman's name? The teacher Golap scolded Paragpawan. Everyone knew that each and every word Paragpawan uttered was true. The dramatist could not stay away from wine. His character was also vile. In inebriated condition he told about his dirty amorous adventures. Everyone knew that he was beaten up by Madhab Pasoni for commenting something bad about his wife. Still some people valued him so much.

"Why don't you tell us Paragpawan whom should we invite instead?" Professor Nripen said to ease up the situation.

"Sir, it's a cultural function on account of **Rangali Bihu**. Moreover, the main attraction of the evening is drumming competition. It will be beneficial if we call an Oja. We always neglect them although the chief instrument of Bihu is **Dhol**." Almost everybody started clapping before Paragpawan could finish his sentence.

According to the decision of the public meeting Paragpawan and other two had come to the house of once famous magician of the **Dhol**, Rangai Oja to invite him to inaugurate first night's cultural competition.

"Our programme will be three days long. During the first two nights there will be various cultural competitions. In the first night there will be the competitions of drumming and whistling of **Pepa**. The competition will start from 6 p.m. Artists from all over Assam will take part in this competition. People from Jorhat have sent us to you with the onus of inviting you to inaugurate the competition that evening."

"You don't have to give speech like other inaugurators. You just have to play on the **Dhol** for a short time. People out there have turned very enthusiastic to know that you will perform on the stage," Parag tried to lure him. He was eagerly looking at his face for an answer. It was his idea to inaugurate the competition with the beatings of **Dhol** rather than any speech. He proposed it in the meeting. Rangai Oja's absent face didn't show any change of expression. His eyes were transfixed outside. Hafiz and others felt uneasy. They were totally at a loss thinking what to do or say and were waiting for him to say something.

Their mother took to bed when we lost the children one after another. She felt giddiness even if she tried to sit down. The words from Rangai Oja's mouth came like a bolt from the blue. All of them felt silent. They just exchanged gazes with each other helplessly.

"What do you mean by lost the children," Paragpawan asked him with a pathetic voice.

The girl was raped by the army personal. Three months later, one night she hanged herself in the jackfruit tree. He went to the door and muttered to himself, "There was the jackfruit tree. She hanged herself there. Later, they had cut it." Listening to Oja's words Paragpawan and two of his friends lips dried up. They sat speechless. Rangai Oja came back and sat in his stool.

"And what happened to the boy?" The words had come out of Apurba's mouth unknowingly. Now they had started to feel the fear. They were actually shivering in fear.

"The boy was shot in his home by unknown killers. Those three were his mates in ULFA. He came home after knowing his sister's incident. He was sitting in his mother's bed and talking. Suddenly three people entered covering their faces with black scarf, dragged him to the yard and shot him there." Rangai Oja again stood up and went to the door and looked at the yard continuously. Paragpawan, Hafiz and Apurba were gazing at the muddy floor in front of them. They felt as if their eyes had become heavy; as if someone had exchanged their eyes with stones. Rangai Oja came back and sat in his stool. He listened to his wife's groan. They felt that their bodies had turned heavy and needed some support to stand up. They had lost words.

We are really very sorry. We have read about the incidents in newspaper. But we did not know that it occurred in your house. Saying this Apurba rubbed his face.

"This is the gift of the Assam government to the poor Assamese people," said Paragpawan and rubbed his tears off. Hafiz could say nothing and kept on gazing at the expressionless bearded face of Rangai Oja.

"Don't be sad. There are thousands of fathers like you throughout Assam. This is the worst government the people of Assam have till now," Paragpawan said. Rangai Oja neither said anything nor showed any expression.

"We will pick you up and drop you back at your home after your work is done. It won't take much time." Apurba said fathering some courage.

"I would have felt very happy, if I could go. I have not beaten the **Dhol** for many years, but....."

"Please, don't say no. People of Jorhat are hoping for your arrival," Paragpawan said with great earnestness.

"Sorry, I can't go. I got many silver medallions. I have sold all one after another. Out of five **Dhol**s, not a single one is left now. Even I don't have a **Khol** also. I have kept a stick as a monument. I have to beat on my bum to perform." Rangai Oja stood up.

Rangai Oja walked in saying that his wife was groaning very much.

What had happened to Paragpawan, Apurba and Hafiz? Why were they sitting on the bench? Why couldn't they talk? Were their eyes working properly?

Glossary

Gamosa: A piece of cloth used for menial chores.

Navapatrika: An object used in sacred contexts.

Bihu: A cultural festival of the Assamese people.

Rangali Bihu: A segment of Bihu festival observed during the spring season.

Dhol: A type of drum.

Pepa: A trombone type musical instrument made of the horns of the buffalo.

Khol: A particular musical instrument used during festivals.

THE END

www.ingramcontent.com/pod-product-compliance
Ingram Content Group UK Ltd.
Pitfield, Milton Keynes, MK11 3LW, UK
UKHW041823200726
13854UKWH00002BA/519